"I'll tell you what," he said. "I'm going to give you a kiss. And if afterward you can walk away, then you should."

She blinked. "I don't want to walk away."

"See how you feel after the kiss."

He already knew.

He already knew that he was going to have a hard time getting his hands off her once they'd been on her.

She took a step toward him, those ridiculous high heels somehow skimming overtop of the dirt and rocks. She was soft and elegant, and he was half dressed and sweaty from chopping wood, his breath a cloud in the cold air.

She reached out and put her hand on his chest. And it took every last ounce of his willpower not to grab her wrist and pin her palm to him. To hold her against him, make her feel the way his heart was beginning to rage out of control.

He couldn't remember the last time he'd wanted a woman like this.

* * *

Rancher's Wild Secret by
New York Times bestselling author Maisey Yates
is part of the Gold Valley Vineyards series.

MAISEY YATES

—

RANCHER'S WILD SECRET

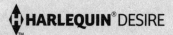

Recycling programs
for this product may
not exist in your area.

ISBN-13: 978-1-335-60397-5

Rancher's Wild Secret

Printed in U.S.A.

In Gold Valley, Oregon, lasting love is only a happily-ever-after away. Don't miss any of Maisey Yates's Gold Valley tales, available now!

For more books by Maisey Yates, visit www.maiseyyates.com.

You can find Maisey Yates on Facebook, along with other Harlequin Desire authors, at www.Facebook.com/harlequindesireauthors!

One

The launch party for Maxfield Vineyards' brand-new select label was going off without a hitch, and Emerson Maxfield was bored.

Not the right feeling for the brand ambassador of Maxfield Vineyards, but definitely the feeling she was battling now.

She imagined many people in attendance would pin the look of disinterest on her face on the fact that her fiancé wasn't present.

She looked down at her hand, currently wrapped around a glass of blush wine, her fourth finger glittering with the large, pear-shaped diamond that she was wearing.

She wasn't bored because Donovan wasn't here.

Frankly, *Donovan* was starting to bore her, and that reality caused her no small amount of concern.

But what else could she do?

Her father had arranged the relationship, the engagement, two years earlier, and she had agreed. She'd been sure that things would progress, that she and Donovan could make it work because on paper they *should* work.

But their relationship wasn't…changing.

They worked and lived in different states and they didn't have enough heat between them to light a campfire.

All things considered, the party was much less boring than her engagement.

But all of it—the party and the engagement—was linked. Linked to the fact that her father's empire was the most important thing in his world.

And Emerson was a part of that empire.

In fairness, she cared about her father. And she cared about his empire, deeply. The winery was her life's work. Helping build it, grow it, was something she excelled at.

She had managed to get Maxfield wines into Hollywood awards' baskets. She'd gotten them recommended on prominent websites by former talk show hosts.

She had made their vineyard label something *better* than local.

Maxfield Vineyards was the leading reason parts of Oregon were beginning to be known as the new Napa.

And her work, and her siblings' work, was the reason Maxfield Vineyards had grown as much as it had.

She should be feeling triumphant about this party.

But instead she felt nothing but malaise.

The same malaise that had infected so much of what she had done recently.

This used to be enough.

Standing in the middle of a beautiful party, wearing a dress that had been hand tailored to conform perfectly to her body—it used to be a thrill. Wearing lipstick like this—the perfect shade of red to go with her scarlet dress—it used to make her feel...

Important.

Like she mattered.

Like everything was put together and polished. Like she was a success. Whatever her mother thought.

Maybe Emerson's problem was the impending wedding.

Because the closer that got, the more doubts she had.

If she could possibly dedicate herself to her job *so much* that she would marry the son of one of the world's most premier advertising executives.

That she would go along with what her father asked, even in this.

But Emerson loved her father. And she loved the winery.

And as for romantic love...

Well, she'd never been in love. It was a hypothetical. But all these other loves were not. And as far as sex and passion went…

She hadn't slept with Donovan yet. But she'd been with two other men. One boyfriend in college, one out of college. And it just hadn't been anything worth upending her life over.

She and Donovan shared goals and values. Surely they could mesh those things together and create a life.

Why not marry for the sake of the vineyard? To make her father happy?

Why not?

Emerson sighed and surveyed the room.

Everything was beautiful. Of course it was. The party was set in her family's gorgeous mountaintop tasting room, the view of the vineyards stretching out below, illuminated by the full moon.

Emerson walked out onto the balcony. There were a few people out there, on the far end, but they didn't approach her. Keeping people at a distance was one of her gifts. With one smile she could attract everyone in the room if she chose. But she could also affect a blank face that invited no conversation at all.

She looked out over the vineyards and sighed yet again.

"What are you doing out here?"

A smile tugged at the corner of Emerson's mouth. Because of course, she could keep everyone but her baby sister Cricket from speaking to her when she didn't want to be spoken to. Cricket basically did what she wanted.

"I just needed some fresh air. What are *you* doing here? Weren't you carded at the door?"

"I'm twenty-one, thank you," Cricket sniffed, looking…well, not twenty-one, at least not to Emerson.

Emerson smirked. "Oh. How could I forget?"

Truly, she *couldn't* forget, as she had thrown an absolutely spectacular party for Cricket, which had made Cricket look wide-eyed and uncomfortable, particularly in the fitted dress Emerson had chosen for her. Cricket did not enjoy being the center of attention.

Emerson *did* like it. But only on her terms.

Cricket looked mildly incensed in the moonlight. "I didn't come out here to be teased."

"I'm sorry," Emerson responded, sincere because she didn't want to hurt her sister. She only wanted to mildly goad her, because Cricket was incredibly goadable.

Emerson looked out across the vast expanse of fields and frowned when she saw a figure moving among the vines.

It was a man. She could tell even from the balcony that he had a lean, rangy body, and the long strides of a man who was quite tall.

"Who's that?" she asked.

"I don't know," Cricket said, peering down below. "Should I get Dad?"

"No," Emerson said. "I can go down."

She knew exactly who was supposed to be at the party, and who wasn't.

And if this man was one of the Coopers from Cowboy Wines, then she would have reason to feel concerned that he was down there sniffing around to get trade secrets.

Not that their top rival had ever stooped to that kind of espionage before, but she didn't trust anyone. Not really.

Wine-making was a competitive industry, and it was only becoming more so.

Emerson's sister Wren always became livid at the mere mention of the Cooper name, and was constantly muttering about all manner of dirty tricks they would employ to get ahead. So really, anything was possible.

"I'll just run down and check it out."

"You're going to go down and investigate by yourself?"

"I'm fine." Emerson waved a hand. "I have a cell phone, and the place is heavily populated right now. I don't think I'm going to have any issues."

"Emerson…"

Emerson slipped back inside, and out a side door, moving quickly down the stairs, not listening to her sister at all. She didn't know why, but she felt compelled to see who the man was for herself.

Maybe because his arrival was the first truly interesting thing to happen all evening. She went in the direction where she'd last seen the figure, stepping out of the golden pool of light spilling from the party and into the grapevines. The moonlight illuminated her steps, though it was pale and left her hands looking waxen.

She rounded one row of grapevines into the next, then stopped, frozen.

She had known he was tall, even from a distance. But he was...very tall. And broad.

Broad shoulders, broad chest. He was wearing a cowboy hat, which seemed ridiculous at night, because it wasn't keeping the sun off him. He had on a tight black T-shirt and a pair of jeans.

And he was not a Cooper.

She had never seen the man before in her life. He saw her and stopped walking. He lifted his head up, and the moonlight caught his features. His face was sculpted, beautiful. So much so that it immobilized her. That square jaw was visible in even this dim light.

"I... Have you lost your way?" she asked. "The party is that way. Though... I'm fairly certain you're not on the guest list."

"I wasn't invited to any party," he said, his voice rough and raspy, made for sin.

Made for sin?

She didn't know where such a thought had come from.

Except, it was easy to imagine that voice saying all kinds of sinful things, and she couldn't credit why.

"Then… Forgive me, but what are you doing here?"

"I work here," he said. "I'm the new ranch hand."

Damn if she wasn't Little Red Riding Hood delivered right to the Big Bad Wolf.

Except, she wasn't wearing a scarlet cloak. It was a scarlet dress that clung to her generous curves like wrapping paper around a tempting present.

Her dark hair was lined silver by the moonbeams and tumbling around naked shoulders.

He could picture her in his bed, just like that. Naked and rumpled in the sheets, that hair spread everywhere.

It was a shame he wasn't here for pleasure.

He was here for revenge.

And if he had guessed correctly based on what he knew about the Maxfield family, this was Emerson Maxfield. Who often had her beautiful face splashed across magazine covers for food and wine features, and who had become something of an It Girl for clothing brands as well. She was gorgeous, recognizable… and engaged.

But none of that would have deterred him, if he really wanted her.

What the hell did he care if a man had put a ring on a woman's finger? In his opinion, if an engaged or married woman was looking elsewhere, then the man who'd put the ring on her finger should've done a better job of keeping her satisfied.

If Holden could seduce a woman, then the bastard he seduced her away from deserved it.

Indiscretion didn't cause him any concern.

But there were a whole lot of women and a whole lot of ways for him to get laid, and he wasn't about to sully himself inside a Maxfield.

No matter how gorgeous.

"I didn't realize my father had hired someone new," she said.

It was funny, given what he knew about her family, the way that she talked like a little private school princess. But he knew she'd gone to elite schools on the East Coast, coming back home to Oregon for summer vacations, at least when her family wasn't jet-setting off somewhere else.

They were the wealthiest family in Logan County, with a wine label that competed on the world stage.

Her father, James Maxfield, was a world-class visionary, a world-class winemaker…and a world-class bastard.

Holden had few morals, but there were some scruples he held dear. At the very top of that list was that when he was with a woman, there was no coercion involved. And he would never leave one hopeless, blackmailed and depressed. No.

But James Maxfield had no such moral code.

And, sadly for James, when it came to dealing out justice to men who had harmed someone Holden cared about very much, he didn't have a limit on how far he was willing to go. He wondered what Emerson would think if she knew what her father had done to a woman who was barely her age.

What he'd done to Holden's younger sister.

But then, Emerson probably wouldn't care at all.

He couldn't see how she would *not* know the way her father behaved, given that the whole family seemed to run the enterprise together.

He had a feeling the Maxfield children looked the other way, as did James's wife. All of them ignoring his bad behavior so they could continue to have access to his bank account.

"I just got here today," he said. "Staying in one of the cabins on the property."

There was staff lodging, which he had found quaint as hell.

Holden had worked his way up from nothing, though his success in real estate development was not anywhere near as splashed over the media as the Maxfield's success was. Which, in the end, was what allowed him to engage in this revenge mission, this quest to destroy the life and reputation of James Maxfield.

And the really wonderful thing was, James wouldn't even see it coming.

Because he wouldn't believe a man of such low status could possibly bring him down. He would overlook Holden. Because James would believe that Holden was nothing more than a hired hand, a lackey.

James would have no idea that Holden was a man

with a massive spread of land in the eastern part of the state, in Jackson Creek.

Because James Maxfield thought of no one but himself. He didn't think anyone was as smart as he was, didn't think anyone was anywhere near as important.

And that pride would be his downfall in the end.

Holden would make sure of it.

"Oh," she said. She met his eyes and bit her lip.

The little vixen was flirting with him.

"Aren't you meant to be in there hosting the party?"

She lifted a shoulder. "I guess so." She didn't seem at all surprised that he recognized who she was. But then, he imagined Emerson was used to being recognized.

"People will probably be noticing that you're gone."

"I suppose they might be," she said. She wrinkled her nose. "Between you and me, I'm getting a little tired of these things."

"Parties with free food and drinks? How could you get tired of that?"

She lifted one elegant shoulder. "I suppose when the drinks are always free, you lose track of why they're special."

"I wouldn't know anything about that."

He'd worked for every damn thing he had.

"Oh. Of course. Sorry. That's an incredibly privileged thing to say."

"Well, if you're who I think you are, you're incredibly privileged. Why wouldn't you feel that way?"

"Just because it's true in my life doesn't mean it's not a tacky thing to say."

"Well, I can think of several tacky things to say right back that might make you feel a little bit better."

She laughed. "Try me."

"If you're not careful, Little Red, wandering through the wilderness like this, a Big Bad Wolf might gobble you up."

It was an incredibly obvious and overtly sexual thing to say. And the little princess, with her engagement ring glittering on her left hand, should have drawn up in full umbrage.

But she didn't. Instead, her body seemed to melt slightly, and she looked away. "Was that supposed to be tacky?"

"It was," he said.

"I guess it didn't feel that way to me."

"You should head back to that party," he said.

"Why? Am I in danger out here?"

"Depends on what you consider danger."

There was nothing wrong—he told himself—with building a rapport with her. In fact, it would be a damned useful thing in many ways.

"Possibly talking to strange men in vineyards."

"Depends on whether or not you consider me strange."

"I don't know you well enough to have that figured out yet." A crackle of interest moved over his skin, and he didn't know what the hell was wrong with him that the first time he'd felt anything remotely like interest in a hell of a long time was happening now.

With Emerson Maxfield.

But she was the one who took a step back. She was the one whose eyes widened in fear, and he had to wonder if his hatred for the blood that ran through her veins was as evident to her as it was to him.

"I have to go," she said. "I'm… The party."

"Yes, ma'am," he said.

He took a step toward her, almost without thinking.

And then she retreated, as quickly as she could on those impractical stiletto heels.

"You better run, Little Red," he said under his breath.

And then he rocked back on his heels, surveying the grapevines and the house up on the hill. "The Big Bad Wolf is going to gobble all of this up."

Two

"Emerson," her dad said. "I have a job for you."

Emerson was tired and feeling off balance after last night. She had done something that was so out of character she still couldn't figure out what she'd been thinking.

She had left the party, left her post. She had chased after a strange man out in the grapevines. And then...

He had reminded her of a wolf. She'd gone to a wolf sanctuary once when she was in high school, and she'd been mesmerized by the powerful pack alpha. So beautiful. So much leashed strength.

She'd been afraid. But utterly fascinated all at once. Unable to look away...

He worked on the property.

And that should have been a red light to her all the way down. An absolute *stop, don't go any further.* If the diamond on her finger couldn't serve as that warning, then his status as an employee should have.

But she had felt drawn to him. And then he'd taken a step toward her. And it was like suddenly the correct instincts had woken up inside of her and she had run away.

But she didn't know why it had taken that long for her to run. What was wrong with her?

"A job," she said blankly, in response to her father.

"I've been watching the profits of Grassroots Winery down in town," he said. "They're really building a name for themselves as a destination. Not just a brand that people drink when they're out, but a place people want to visit. We've proved this is an incredibly successful location for weddings and other large events. The party you threw last night was superb."

Emerson basked in the praise. But only for a moment. Because if there was praise, then a request couldn't be far behind.

"One of the things they're offering is rides through the vineyard on horseback. They're also doing sort of a rustic partnership with the neighboring dude ranch, which sounds more like the bastion of Cowboy Wines. Nothing I want to get involved with. We don't want to lower the value of our brand by associating with anything down-market. But horse rides through the vineyards, picnics, things like that—I think those could be profitable."

Emerson had met the owner of Grassroots Winery, Lindy Dodge, on a couple of occasions, and she liked the other woman quite a lot. Emerson had a moment of compunction about stepping on what had clearly been Lindy's idea, but then dismissed it.

It wasn't uncommon at all for similar companies to try comparable ventures. They often borrowed from each other, and given the number of wineries beginning to crop up in the area, it was inevitable there would be crossover.

Plus, to the best of her ability Emerson tried not to look at the others as competition. They were creating a robust wine trail that was a draw in and of itself.

Tourists could visit several wineries when they came to Logan County, traveling from Copper Ridge through Gold Valley and up into the surrounding mountains. That the area was a destination for wine enthusiasts was good for everyone.

The only vineyard that Maxfield Vineyards really viewed as competition was Cowboy Wines. Which Emerson thought was funny in a way, since their brand could not be more disparate from Maxfield's if they tried.

And she suspected they *did* try.

She also suspected there was something darker at the root of the rivalry, but if so, James never said.

And neither had Wren, the middle sister. Wren's role in the company often saw her clashing with Creed Cooper, who worked in the same capacity for his family winery, and Wren hated him with every fiber of her being. Loudly and often.

"So what is the new venture exactly?" Emerson asked.

"I just told you. Trail rides and picnics, but we need a way to make it feel like a Maxfield endeavor. And that, I give over to you."

"That sounds like it would be more Wren's thing." Wren was responsible for events at the winery, while Emerson dealt more globally with brand representation.

"I think ultimately this will be about the way you influence people. I want you to find the best routes, the prime views for the trips, take some photos, put it up on your social media. Use the appropriate pound signs."

"It's a... It's a hashtag."

"I'm not interested in learning what it is, Emerson. That's why I have you."

"Okay. I can do that."

She did have a massive online reach, and she could see how she might position some photos, which would garner media interest, and possibly generate a story in *Sip and Savor* magazine. And really, it would benefit the entire area. The more that Maxfield Vineyards—with its vast reach in the world of wine—brought people into the area, the more the other vineyards benefited too.

"That sounds good to me," she said.

"That's why I hired a manager for the ranching

portion of the facility. I need him to oversee some new construction, because if we're going to have guests in the stables, everything needs to be updated. I need for him to oversee the acquisition of a few horses. Plus, the rides, etc."

"Oh," she said. "This…person. This man you hired. He's…tall?"

James shrugged. "I don't know. I didn't consider his height. Did you?"

"No," she said, her face flaming. She felt like a child with her hand caught in the cookie jar. "I just… I think I saw him last night. Down in the vineyard. I left the party to check and see what was happening." Total honesty with her father came as second nature to her.

She tried to be good. She tried to be the daughter he had raised her to be, always.

"You left the party?"

"Everything was well in hand. I left Cricket in charge."

That might be a stretch. But while she was as honest with her father as possible, she tended to leave out some things like…her feelings. And this would be one of those times.

"I met him briefly, then I went back to the house. That's all. He told me he worked on the property."

"You have to be careful," her father said. "You don't want any photographs taken of you alone with a man who's not Donovan. You don't need anything to compromise your engagement."

Sometimes she wondered if her father realized they didn't live in the Victorian era.

"Nothing is going to compromise my engagement to Donovan."

"I'm glad you're certain about it."

She was, in spite of her occasional doubts. Her father might not understand that times had changed, but she did. She felt certain Donovan was carrying on with other women in the absence of a physical relationship with her. Why would she assume anything else? He was a man, after all.

She knew why her father was so invested in her marriage to Donovan. As part of his planned retirement, her father was giving ownership stakes in the winery to each of his daughters' husbands.

He felt Donovan would be an asset to the winery, and Emerson agreed. But she wasn't sure how that fit into a marriage.

Clearly, Donovan didn't much care about how that fit into a marriage either.

And she doubted he would be able to muster up any jealousy over her behavior.

"Image," her father said, bringing her back to the moment. "It isn't what you do that matters, Emerson, it's what the world *thinks* you're doing."

There was something about the way her father said it, so smooth and cold, that made her feel chilled. It shouldn't chill her, because she agreed that image was important in their business.

Still, it *did* chill her.

Emerson shifted. "Right. Well, no worries there. Image is my expertise."

"It's all about the brand," he said.

"I tell you that," she said.

"And you've done it well."

"Thank you," she said, nearly flushed with pleasure. Compliments from James Maxfield were rare, and she clung to them when she got them.

"You should head down to the stables. He'll be waiting for you."

And if that made her stomach tighten, she ignored the sensation. She had a job to do. And that job had nothing to do with how tall the new ranch manager was.

She was as pretty in the ridiculously trendy outfit she was wearing now as she'd been in that red dress.

She was wearing high-cut black pants that went up past her belly button, loose fitted through the leg, with a cuff around the ankle, paired with a matching black top that was cropped to just beneath her breasts and showed a wedge of stomach. Her dark hair was in a high bun, and she was wearing the same red lipstick she'd had on the night before, along with round sunglasses that covered her eyes.

He wished he could see her eyes. And as she approached, she pushed the glasses up to the top of her head.

He hadn't been prepared for how beautiful she was.

He thought he'd seen her beauty in the moonlight,

thought he'd seen it in photographs, but they didn't do her justice. He'd been convinced that the blue of her eyes was accomplished with some kind of a filter. But it was clear to him now, out in the bright sun with the green mountains surrounding them, and her eyes reflecting that particular blue from the center of the sky, that if anything, her eyes had been downplayed in those photographs.

"Good morning," she said.

"Good morning to you too. I take it you spoke with your father?"

It took all of his self-control for that word to come out smoothly.

"Yes," she said. "I did."

"And what do you think of his proposition?"

In Holden's opinion, it was a good one. And when he was through ruining James and sinking his brand, Holden might well buy the entire property and continue making wine himself. He was good at selling things, making money. He could make more money here.

"It's good. I think a few well-placed selfies will drum up interest."

"You're probably right. Though, I can't say I'm real up on selfies."

That was a lie. His younger sister was a pretty powerful influencer. A model, who had met James Maxfield at one of the parties that had brought their type together. He was angry at himself for the part his own money had played in all of this.

Because Soraya had been innocent. A sweet girl from a small town who had been catapulted into a lifestyle she hadn't been prepared to handle.

Holden could relate well enough.

He certainly hadn't known how to handle money in the beginning.

But he'd been helping his family dig out of the hole they'd found themselves in. The first thing he'd done was buy his mother a house. Up on a hill, fancy and safe from the men who had used her all throughout Holden's childhood.

And his sweet, younger half sister… She'd tumbled headfirst into fame. She was beautiful, that much had always been apparent, but she had that lean, hungry kind of beauty, honed by years of poverty, her backstory lending even more interest to her sharp cheekbones and unerring sense of style.

She had millions of people following her, waiting to see her next picture. Waiting to see which party she would attend.

And she attended the wrong one when she met James Maxfield.

He'd pounced on her before Holden could say "daddy issues." And James had left her devastated. Holden would never forget having to admit his sister for a psychiatric hold. Soraya's suicide attempt, the miscarriage… The devastation.

It was burned in him.

Along with the reality that his money hadn't protected her. His money had opened her up to this.

Now all that was left was revenge, because he couldn't make it right. He couldn't take her pain away.

But he could take everything away from the Maxfield family.

And that was what he intended to do.

"I don't think we've officially met," she said. She stuck her hand out—the one that didn't have the ring on it. That one angled at her side, the gem sparkling in the sunlight. "I'm Emerson Maxfield."

"Holden Brown," he said, extending his own hand.

If James Maxfield weren't a raging narcissist, Holden might have worried about using his real first name.

But he doubted the older man would ever connect the younger model he'd used for a couple of months and then discarded with Holden. Why would he? James probably barely remembered Soraya's first name, much less any of her family connections. Holden himself wasn't famous. And that was how he liked it. He'd always thought it would be handy to have anonymity. He hadn't imagined it would be for reasons of revenge.

He closed his hand around hers. It was soft, desperately so. The hand of a woman who had never done hard labor in her life, and something in him suddenly felt desperate to make this little princess do some down and dirty work.

Preferably on his body.

He pulled his hand away.

"It's nice to meet you, Holden," she said.

"Nice to meet you too." He bit the pleasantry off at the end, because anything more and he might make a mistake.

"I have some routes in mind for this new venture. Let's go for a ride."

Three

Let's go for a ride was not sexual.

Not in the context of the ranch. Not to a woman who was so used to being exposed to horses. As she was.

Except, she kept replaying that line over and over in her head. Kept imagining herself saying it to him.

Let's go for a ride.

And then she would imagine herself saying it to him in bed.

She had never, ever felt like this in her entire life.

Her first time had been fine. Painless, which was nice, she supposed, but not exactly exciting.

It had been with her boyfriend at the time, who she'd known very well, and who had been extraordinarily careful and considerate.

Though, he'd cared more about keeping her comfortable than keeping her impassioned. But they had been young. So that seemed fair enough.

Her boyfriend after that had been smooth, urbane and fascinating to her. A world traveler before she had done any traveling of her own. She had enjoyed conversations with him, but she hadn't been consumed by passion or lust or anything like that.

She had just sort of thought she was that way. And she was fine with it. She had a lot of excitement in her life. She wasn't hurting for lack of passion.

But Holden made her feel like she might actually be missing something.

Like there was a part of herself that had been dormant for a very long time.

Right. You've been in the man's presence for...a combined total of forty minutes.

Well, that made an even stronger case for the idea of exploring the thing between them. Because in that combined forty minutes, she had imagined him naked at least six times.

Had thought about closing the distance between them and kissing him on the mouth no less than seven times.

And that was insane.

He was working on the ranch, working for her father. Working for her, in essence, as she was part of the winery and had a stake in the business.

And somehow, that aroused her even more.

A man like her fiancé, Donovan, knew a whole lot about the world.

He knew advertising, and there was a heck of a lot of human psychology involved in that. And it was interesting.

But she had a feeling that a man like Holden could teach her about her own body, and that was more than interesting. It was a strange and intoxicating thought.

Also, totally unrealistic and nothing you're going to act on.

No, she thought as she mounted her horse, and the two of them began riding along a trail that she wanted to investigate as a route for the new venture. She would never give in to this just for the sake of exploring her sensuality. For a whole list of reasons.

So you're just going to marry Donovan and wonder what this could have been like?

Sink into the mediocre sex life that the lack of attraction between you promises. Never know what you're missing.

Well, the thing about fantasies was they were only fantasies.

And the thing about sex with a stranger—per a great many of her friends who'd had sex with strangers—was that the men involved rarely lived up to the fantasy. Because they had no reason to make anything good for a woman they didn't really know.

They were too focused on making it good for themselves. And men always won in those games.

Emerson knew her way around her own body, knew how to find release when she needed it. But she'd yet to find a man who could please her in the same way, and when she was intimate with someone, she couldn't ever quite let go... There were just too many things to think about, and her brain was always consumed.

It wouldn't be different with Holden. No matter how hot he was.

And blowing up all her inhibitions over an experience that was bound to be a letdown was something Emerson simply wasn't going to risk.

So there.

She turned her thoughts away from the illicit and forced them onto the beauty around her.

Her family's estate had been her favorite place in the world since she was a child. But of course, when she was younger, that preference had been a hollow kind of favoritism, because she didn't have a wide array of experiences or places to compare it to.

She did now. She'd been all over the world, had stayed in some of the most amazing hotels, had enjoyed food in the most glamorous locales. And while she loved to travel, she couldn't imagine a time when she wouldn't call Maxfield Vineyards home.

From the elegant spirals of the vines around the wooden trellises, all in neat rows spreading over vast acres, to the manicured green lawns, to the farther reaches where it grew wild, the majestic beauty of the wilderness so big and awe-inspiring, making her feel appropriately small and insignificant when the occasion required.

"Can I ask you a question?" His voice was deep and thick, like honey, and it made Emerson feel like she was on the verge of a sugar high.

She'd never felt anything like this before.

This, she supposed, was chemistry. And she couldn't for the life of her figure out why it would suddenly be *this* man who inspired it. She had met so many men who weren't so far outside the sphere of what she should find attractive. She'd met them at parties all around the world. None of those men—including the one her father wanted her to be engaged to—had managed to elicit this kind of response in her.

And yet… Holden did it effortlessly.

"Ask away," she said, resolutely fixing her focus on the scene around them. Anything to keep from fixating on him.

"Why the hell did you wear *that* knowing we were going out riding?"

She blinked. Then she turned and looked at him. "What's wrong with my outfit?"

"I have never seen anyone get on a horse in something so impractical."

"Oh, come now. Surely you've seen period pieces where the woman is in a giant dress riding sidesaddle."

"Yes," he said. "But you have other options."

"It has to be photographable," she said.

"And you couldn't do some sexy cowgirl thing?"

Considering he was playing the part of sexy cowboy—in his tight black T-shirt and black cowboy hat—she suddenly wished she were playing the part of sexy cowgirl. Maybe with a plaid top knotted just beneath her breasts, some short shorts and cowgirl boots. Maybe, if she were in an outfit like that, she would feel suitably bold enough to ask him for a literal roll in the hay.

You've lost your mind.

"That isn't exactly my aesthetic."

"Your aesthetic is… *I Dream of Jeannie* in Mourning?"

She laughed. "I hadn't thought about it that way. But sure. *I Dream of Jeannie* in Mourning sounds about right. In fact, I think I might go ahead and label the outfit that when I post pics."

"Whatever works," he said.

His comment was funny. And okay, maybe the fact that he'd been clever a couple of times in her presence was bestowing the label of *funny* on him too early. But it made her feel a little bit better about her wayward hormones that he wasn't just beautiful, that he was fascinating as well.

"So today's ride isn't just a scouting mission for you," he said. "If you're worried about your aesthetic."

"No," she said. "I want to start generating interest in this idea. You know, pictures of me on the horse. In fact, hang on a second." She stopped, maneuvering her mount, turning so she was facing Holden, with the brilliant backdrop of the trail and the mountains behind them. Then she flipped her phone front facing and raised it up in the air, tilting it downward and grinning as she hit the button. She looked at the result, frowned, and then did it again. The second one would be fine once she put some filters on it.

"What was that?"

She maneuvered her horse back around in the other direction, stuffed her phone in her pocket and carried on.

"It was me getting a photograph," she said. "One that I can post. 'Something new and exciting is coming to the Maxfield label.'"

"Are you really going to put it like that?"

"Yes. I mean, eventually we'll do official press releases and other forms of media, but the way you use social media advertisements is a little different. I personally am part of that online brand. And my lifestyle—including my clothes—is part of what makes people interested in the vineyard."

"Right," he said.

"People want to be jealous," she said. "If they didn't, they wouldn't spend hours scrolling through photos of other people's lives. Or of houses they'll never be able to live in. Exotic locations they'll never be able to go. A little envy, that bit of aspiration, it drives some people."

"Do you really believe that?"

"Yes. I think the success of my portion of the family empire suggests I know what I'm talking about."

He didn't say anything for a long moment. "You know, I suppose you're right. People choose to indulge in that feeling, but when you really don't have anything, it's not fun to see all that stuff you'll never have. It cuts deep. It creates a hunger, rather than enjoyment. It can drive some people to the edge of destruction."

There was something about the way he said it that sent a ripple of disquiet through her. Because his words didn't sound hypothetical.

"That's never my goal," she said. "And I can't control who consumes the media I put out there. At a certain point, people have to know themselves, don't they?"

"True enough," he said. "But some people don't. And it's worse when there's another person involved who sees weakness in them even when they don't see it themselves. Someone who exploits that weakness. Plenty of sad, hungry girls have been lost along that envious road, when they took the wrong hand desperate for a hand up into satisfaction."

"Well, I'm not selling wild parties," she said. "I'm selling an afternoon ride at a family winery, and a trip here is not that out of reach for most people. That's the thing. There's all this wild aspirational stuff out there online, and the vineyard is just a little more accessible. That's what makes it advertising and not luxury porn."

"I see. Create a desire so big it can never be filled, and then offer a winery as the consolation prize."

"If the rest of our culture supports that, it's hardly my fault."

"Have you ever had to want for anything in your entire life, Emerson?" The question was asked innocuously enough, but the way he asked it, in that dark, rough voice, made it buzz over her skin, crackling like electricity as it moved through her. "Or have you always been given everything you could ever desire?"

"I've wanted things," she said, maybe too quickly. Too defensively.

"What?" he pressed.

She desperately went through the catalog of her life, trying to come up with a moment when she had been denied something that she had wanted in a material sense. And there was only one word that burned in her brain.

You.

Yes, that was what she would say. *I want you, and I can't have you. Because I'm engaged to a man who's not interested in kissing me, much less getting into bed with me. And I'm no more interested in doing that with him.*

But I can't break off the engagement no matter how much I want to because I so desperately need...

"Approval," she said. "That's...that's something I want."

Her stomach twisted, and she kept her eyes fixed

ahead, because she didn't know why she had let the word escape out loud. She should have said nothing.

He wasn't interested in hearing about her emotional issues.

"From your father?" he asked.

"No," she said. "I have his approval. My mother, on the other hand…"

"You're famous, successful, beautiful. And you don't have your mother's approval?"

"Yeah, shockingly, my mother's goal for me wasn't to take pictures of myself and put them up on the internet."

"Unless you have a secret stash of pictures, I don't see how your mother could disapprove of these sorts of photographs. Unless, of course, it's your pants. Which I do think are questionable."

"These are *wonderful* pants. And actually deceptively practical. Because they allow me to sit on the horse comfortably. Whatever you might think."

"What doesn't your mother approve of?"

"She wanted me to do something more. Something that was my own. She doesn't want me just running publicity for the family business. But I like it. I enjoy what I do, I enjoy this brand. Representing it is easy for me, because I care about it. I went to school for marketing, close to home. She felt like it was…limiting my potential."

He chuckled. "I'm sorry. Your mother felt like you limited your potential by going to get a degree in marketing and then going on to be an ambassador for a successful brand."

"Yes," she said.

She could still remember the brittle irritation in her mother's voice when she had told her about the engagement to Donovan.

"So you're marrying a man more successful in advertising in the broader world even though you could have done that."

"You're married to a successful man."

"I was never given the opportunities that you were given. You don't have to hide behind a husband's shadow. You could've done more."

"Yeah, that's about the size of it," she said. "Look, my mother is brilliant. And scrappy. And I respect her. But she's never going to be overly impressed with me. As far as she's concerned, I haven't worked a day in my life for anything, and I took the path of least resistance into this version of success."

"What does she think of your sisters?"

"Well, Wren works for the winery too, but the only thing that annoys my mother more than her daughters taking a free pass is the Cooper family, and since Wren makes it her life's work to go toe-to-toe with them, my mother isn't quite as irritated with everything Wren does. And Cricket… I don't know that anyone knows what Cricket wants."

Poor Cricket was a later addition to the family. Eight years younger than Emerson, and six years younger than Wren. Their parents hadn't planned on having another child, and they especially hadn't planned on one like Cricket, who didn't seem to have inherited the need to please…well, anyone.

Cricket had run wild over the winery, raised more by the staff than by their mother or father.

Sometimes Emerson envied Cricket and the independence she seemed to have found before turning twenty-one, when Emerson couldn't quite capture independence even at twenty-nine.

"Sounds to me like your mother is pretty difficult to please."

"Impossible," she agreed.

But her father wasn't. He was proud of her. She was doing exactly what he wanted her to do. And she would keep on doing it.

The trail ended in a grassy clearing on the side of the mountain, overlooking the valley below. The wineries rolled on for miles, and the little redbrick town of Gold Valley was all the way at the bottom.

"Yes," she said. "This is perfect." She got down off the horse, snapped another few pictures with herself in them and the view in the background. And then a sudden inspiration took hold, and she whipped around quickly, capturing the blurred outline of Holden, on his horse with his cowboy hat, behind her.

He frowned, dismounting the horse, and she looked into the phone screen, keeping her eyes on him, and took another shot. He was mostly a silhouette, but it was clear that he was a good-looking, well-built man in a cowboy hat.

"Now, *there's* an ad," she said.

"What're you doing?"

He sounded angry. Not amused at all.

"I just thought it would be good to get you in the background. A full-on Western fantasy."

"You said that wasn't the aesthetic."

"It's not mine. Just because a girl doesn't want to wear cutoff shorts doesn't mean she's not interested in looking at a cowboy."

"You can't post that," he said, his voice hard like granite.

She turned to face him. "Why not?"

"Because I don't want to be on your bullshit website."

"It's not a website. It's… Never mind. Are you… You're not, like, fleeing from the law or something, are you?"

"No," he said. "I'm not."

"Then why won't you let me post your picture? It's not like you can really see you."

"I'm not interested in that stuff."

"Well, that stuff is my entire life's work." She turned her focus to the scenery around them and pretended to be interested in taking a few random pictures that were not of him.

"Some website that isn't going to exist in a couple of years is not your life's work. Your life's work might be figuring out how to sell things to people, advertising, marketing. Whatever you want to call it. But the *how* of it is going to change, and it's going to keep on changing. What you've done is figure out how to understand the way people discover things right now. But it will change. And you'll figure that out too. These pictures are not your life's work."

It was an impassioned speech, and one she almost felt certain he'd given before, though she couldn't quite figure out why he would have, or to who.

"That's nice," she said. "But I don't need a pep talk. I wasn't belittling myself. I won't post the pictures. Though, I think they would have caused a lot of excitement."

"I'm not going to be anyone's trail guide. So there's no point using me."

"You're not even *my* trail guide, not really." She turned to face him, and found he was much closer than she had thought. All the breath was sucked from her body. He was so big and broad, imposing.

There was an intensity about him that should repel her, but instead it fascinated her.

The air was warm, and she was a little bit sweaty, and that made her wonder if *he* was sweaty, and something about that thought made her want to press her face against his chest and smell his skin.

"Have you ever gone without something?"

She didn't know why she'd asked him that, except that maybe it was the only thing keeping her from actually giving in to her fantasy and pressing her face against his body.

"I don't really think that's any of your business."

"Why not? I just downloaded all of my family issues onto you, and I'm not even sure why. Except that you asked. And I don't think anyone else has ever asked. So… It's just you and me out here."

"And your phone. Which is your link to the outside world on a scale that I can barely understand."

Somehow, that rang false.

"I don't have service," she said. "And anyway, my phone is going back in my pocket." She slipped it into the silky pocket of her black pants.

He looked at her, his dark eyes moving over her body, and she knew he was deliberately taking his time examining her curves. Knew that his gaze was deliberately sexual.

And she didn't feel like she could be trusted with that kind of knowledge, because something deep inside her was dancing around the edge of being bold. That one little piece of her that felt repressed, that had felt bored at the party last night…

That one little piece of her wanted this.

"A few things," he said slowly. And his words were deliberate too.

Without thinking, she sucked her lip between her teeth and bit down on it, then swiped her tongue over the stinging surface to soothe it.

And the intensity in his eyes leaped higher.

She couldn't pretend she didn't know what she'd done. She'd deliberately drawn his focus to her mouth.

Now, she might have done it deliberately, but she didn't know what she wanted out of it.

Well, she did. But she couldn't want *that*. She couldn't. Not when…

Suddenly, he reached out, grabbing her chin between his thumb and forefinger. "I don't know how the boys who run around in your world play, Emerson. But I'm not a man who scrolls through photos and wishes he could touch something. If I want something, I take it. So if I were you…I wouldn't go around teasing."

She stuttered, "I… I… I…" and stumbled backward. She nearly tripped down onto the grass, onto her butt, but he reached out, looping his strong arm around her waist and pulling her upright. The breath whooshed from her lungs, and she found herself pressed hard against his solid body. She put her hand gingerly on his chest. Yeah. He was a little bit sweaty.

And damned if it wasn't sexy.

She racked her brain, trying to come up with something witty to say, something to defuse the situation, but she couldn't think. Her heart was thundering fast, and there was an echoing pulse down in the center of her thighs making it impossible for her to breathe. Impossible for her to think. She felt like she was having an out-of-body experience, or a wild fantasy that was surely happening in her head only, and not in reality.

But his body was hot and hard underneath her hand, and there was a point at which she really couldn't pretend she wasn't touching an actual man.

Because her fingers burned. Because her body burned. Because everything burned.

And she couldn't think of a single word to say, which wasn't like her, but usually she wasn't affected by men.

They liked her. They liked to flirt and talk with her, and since becoming engaged, they'd only liked it even more. Seeing her as a bit of a challenge, and it didn't cost her anything to play into that a little bit. Because she was never tempted to do anything. Because she was never affected. Because it was only ever a conversation and nothing more.

But this felt like more.

The air was thick with *more*, and she couldn't figure out why him, why now.

His lips curved up into a half smile, and suddenly, in a brief flash, she saw it.

Sure, his sculpted face and body were part of it. But he was…an outlaw.

Everything she wasn't.

He was a man who didn't care at all what anyone thought. It was visible in every part of him. In the laconic grace with which he moved, the easy way he smiled, the slow honeyed timbre of his voice.

Yes.

He was a man without a cell phone.

A man who wasn't tied or tethered to anything. Who didn't have comments to respond to at two in the morning that kept him up at night, as he worried about not doing it fast enough, about doing something to damage the very public image she had cultivated—not just for herself—but for her father's entire industry.

A man who didn't care if he fell short of the expectations of a parent, at least he didn't seem like he would.

Looking at him in all his rough glory, the way that he blended into the terrain, she felt like a smooth shiny shell with nothing but a sad, listless urchin curled up inside, who was nothing like the facade that she presented.

He was the real deal.

He was like that mountain behind him. Strong and firm and steady. Unmovable.

It made her want a taste.

A taste of him.

A taste of freedom.

She found herself moving forward, but he took a step back.

"Come on now, princess," he said, grabbing hold of her left hand and raising it up, so that her ring caught the sunlight. "You don't want to be doing that."

Horror rolled over her and she stepped away.

"I don't… Nothing."

He chuckled. "Something."

"I… My fiancé and I have an understanding," she said. And she made a mental note to actually check with Donovan to see if they did. Because she suspected they might, given that they had never touched each other. And she could hardly imagine that Donovan had been celibate for the past two years.

You have been.

Yeah, she needed to check on the Donovan thing.

"Do you now?"

"Yes," she lied.

"Well, I have an understanding with your father that I'm in his employment. And I would sure hate to take advantage of that."

"I'm a grown woman," she said.

"Yeah, what do you suppose your daddy would think if he found that you were fucking the help?"

Heat washed over her, her scalp prickling.

"I don't keep my father much informed about my sex life," she said.

"The problem is, you and me would be his business. I try to make my sex life no one's business but mine and the lady I'm naked with."

"Me nearly kissing you is not the same as me offering you sex. Your ego betrays you."

"And your blush betrays you, darlin'."

The entire interaction felt fraught and spiky, and Emerson didn't know how to proceed, which was as rare as her feeling at a loss for words. He was right. He worked for her father, and by extension, for the family, for her. But she didn't feel like she had the power here. Didn't feel like she had the control. She was the one with money, with the Maxfield family name, and he was just...a *ranch hand*.

So why did she feel so decidedly at a disadvantage?

"We'd better carry on," she said. "I have things to do."

"Pictures to post."

"But not of you," she said.

He shook his head once. "Not of me."

She got back on her horse, and he did the same. And this time he led the way back down the trail, and she was somewhat relieved. Because she didn't know what she would do if she had to bear the burden of knowing he was watching the back of her the whole way.

She would drive herself crazy thinking about how to hold her shoulders so that she didn't look like she knew that he was staring at her.

But then, maybe he wouldn't stare at her, and that was the thing. She would wonder either way. And she didn't particularly want to wonder.

And when she got back to her office, she tapped her fingers on the desk next to her phone, and did her very best to stop herself from texting Donovan.

Tap. *Don't.* Tap. *Don't.*

And then suddenly she picked up the phone and started a new message.

Are we exclusive?

There were no dots, no movement. She set the phone down and tried to look away. It pinged a few minutes later.

We are engaged.

That's not an answer.

We don't live in the same city.

She took a breath.

Have you slept with someone else?

She wasn't going to wait around with his back-and-forth nonsense. She wasn't interested in him sparing himself repercussions.

We don't live in the same city. So yes, I have.

And if I did?

Whatever you do before the wedding is your business.

She didn't respond, and his next text came in on the heels of the last.

Did you want to talk on the phone?

No.

K.

And that was it. Because they didn't love each other. She hadn't needed to text him, because nothing was going to happen with her and Holden.

And how do you feel about the fact that Donovan had slept with other people?

She wasn't sure.

Except she didn't feel much of anything.

Except now she had a get-out-of-jail-free card, and that was about the only way she could see it. That wasn't normal, was it? It wasn't normal for him to be okay with the fact that she had asked those questions. That she had made it clear she'd thought about sleeping with someone else.

And it wasn't normal for her to not be jealous when Donovan said he *had* slept with someone else.

But she wasn't jealous.

And his admission didn't dredge any deep feelings up to the surface either.

No, her reaction just underlined the fact that something was missing from their arrangement. Which she had known. Neither of them was under the impression they were in a real relationship. They had allowed themselves to be matched, but before this moment she had been sure feelings would grow in time, but they hadn't, and she and Donovan had ignored that.

But she couldn't...

Her father didn't ask much of her. And he gave her endless support. If she disappointed him...

Well, then she would be a failure all around, wouldn't she?

He's not choosing Wren's husband. He isn't choosing Cricket's.

Well, Wren would likely refuse. Emerson couldn't imagine her strong-headed sister giving in to that. And Cricket… Well, nobody could tame Cricket.

Her father hadn't asked them. He'd asked her. And she'd agreed, because that was who she was. She was the one who could be counted on for anything, and it was too late to stop being who she was now.

Texting Donovan had been insane, leaning in toward Holden had been even more insane. And she didn't have time for any of that behavior. She had a campaign to launch and she was going to do it. Because she knew who she was. She was not the kind of person who kissed men she barely knew, not the kind of person who engaged in physical-only flings, not the kind of person who crossed professional boundaries.

The problem was, Holden made her feel very, very *not* like herself. And that was the most concerning thing of all.

Four

Emerson was proving to be deeply problematic.

What he should do was go down to the local bar and find himself a woman to pick up. Because God knew he didn't need to be running around getting hard over his enemy's daughter. He had expected to be disgusted by everything the Maxfield family was. And indeed, when he had stood across from James Maxfield in the man's office while interviewing for this position, it had taken every ounce of Holden's willpower not to fly across the desk and strangle the man to death.

The thing was, death would be too easy an out for a man like him. Holden would rather give James the full experience of degradation in life before he consigned him to burning in hell for all eternity. Holden wanted to maximize the punishment.

Hell could wait.

And hell was no less than he deserved.

Holden had finally gotten what he'd come for.

It had come in the form of nondisclosure agreements he'd found in James's office. He'd paid attention to the code on the door when James had let him in for the interview, and all he'd had to do was wait for a time when the man was out and get back in there.

It fascinated Holden that everything was left unguarded, but it wasn't really a mystery.

This was James's office in his family home. Not a corporate environment. He trusted his family, and why wouldn't he? It was clear that Emerson had nothing but good feelings about her father. And Holden suspected everyone else in the household felt the same.

Except the women James had coerced into bed. Employees. All young. All dependent on him for a paycheck. But he'd sent them off with gag orders and payoffs.

And once Holden figured out exactly how to approach this, James would be finished.

But now there was the matter of Emerson.

Holden hadn't expected the attraction that had flared up immediately the first time he'd seen her not to let up.

And she was always…around. The problem with

taking on a job as an opportunity to commit corporate espionage, and to find proof either of monetary malfeasance or of the relationship between James and Holden's sister, was that he had to actually *work* during the day.

That ate up a hell of a lot of his time. It also meant he was in close proximity to Emerson.

And speak of the devil, right as he finished mucking out a stall, she walked in wearing skintight tan breaches that molded to every dimple of her body.

"That's a different sort of riding getup," he said.

"I'm not taking selfies today," she said, a teasing gleam in her blue eyes that made his gut tight.

"Just going on a ride?"

"I needed to clear my head," she said.

She looked at him, seeming vaguely edgy.

"What is it?"

But he knew what it was. It was that attraction that he felt every time she was near. She felt it too, and that made it a damn sight worse.

"Nothing. I just… What is it that you normally do? Are you always a ranch hand? I mean, you must specialize in something, or my father wouldn't have hired you to help with the horses."

"I'm good with horses."

Most everything he'd said about himself since coming to the winery was a lie. But this, at least, was true. He had grown up working other people's ranches.

Now he happened to own one of his own, a good-sized spread, but he still did a portion of the labor. He liked working his own land. It was a gift, after so many years of working other people's.

If there was work to be given over to others, he preferred to farm out his office work, not the ranch work.

He'd found an affinity with animals early on, and that had continued. It had given him something to do, given him something to *be*.

He had been nothing but a poor boy from a poor family. He'd been a cowboy from birth. That connection with animals had gotten him his first job at a ranch, and that line of work had gotten him where he was today.

When one of his employers had died, he'd gifted Holden with a large plot of land. It wasn't his ranch, but totally dilapidated fields a few miles from the ranch he now owned.

He hadn't known what the hell to do with land so undeveloped at first, until he'd gone down to the county offices and found it could be divided. From there, he'd started working with a developer.

Building a subdivision had been an interesting project, because a part of him had hated the idea of turning a perfectly good stretch of land into houses. But then, another part of him had enjoyed the fact that new houses meant more people would experience the land he loved and the town he called home.

Making homes for families felt satisfying.

As a kid who had grown up without one at times,

he didn't take for granted the effect four walls could have on someone's life.

And that had been a bargain he'd struck with the developer. That a couple of the homes were his to do with as he chose. They'd been gifted to homeless families going on ten years ago now. And each of the children had been given college scholarships, funded by his corporation now that he was more successful.

He'd done the same ever since, with every development he'd created. It wouldn't save the whole world, but it changed the lives of the individuals involved. And he knew well enough what kind of effect that change could have on a person.

He'd experienced it himself.

Cataloging everything good you've done in the past won't erase what you're doing now.

Maybe not. But he didn't much care. Yes, destroying the Maxfield empire would sweep Emerson right up in his revenge, which was another reason he'd thought it might be more convenient to hate everyone connected with James Maxfield.

He'd managed to steer clear of the youngest daughter, Cricket, who always seemed to be flitting in and out of the place, and he'd seen Wren on many occasions, marching around purposefully, but he hadn't quite figured out exactly what her purpose was. Nor did he want to.

But Emerson… Emerson he couldn't seem to stay away from. Or maybe she couldn't stay away from him. At the end of it all, he didn't know if it mattered which it was.

They kept colliding either way.

"You must be very good with horses," she said.

"I don't know about that. But I was here, available to do the job, so your father gave it to me."

She tilted her head to the side, appraising him like he was a confusing piece of modern art. "Are you married?"

"Hell no," he said. "No desire for that kind of nonsense."

"You think love is nonsense?" she pressed.

"You didn't ask me about love. You asked me about marriage."

"Don't they usually go together?"

"Does it for you? Because you nearly kissed me yesterday, and you're wearing another man's ring."

Great. He'd gone and brought that up. Not a good idea, all things considered. Though, it might make her angry, and if he could get her good and angry, that might be for the best.

Maybe then she would stay away.

"I told you, we're not living near each other right now, so we…have an arrangement."

"So you said. But what does that mean?"

"We are not exclusive."

"Then what the hell is the point of being engaged? As I understand it, the only reason to put a ring on a woman's finger is to make her yours. Sure and certain. If you were my woman, I certainly wouldn't let another man touch you."

Her cheeks flushed red. "Well, you certainly have a lot of opinions for someone who doesn't see a point to the institution of marriage."

"Isn't the point *possession*?"

"Women aren't seen as cattle anymore. So no."

"I didn't mean a woman being a possession. The husband and wife possess each other. Isn't that the point?"

She snorted. "I think that often the point is dynasty and connections, don't you?"

"Damn, that's cynical, even for me."

She ignored that. "So, you're good with horses, and you don't believe in marriage," she said. "Anything else?"

"Not a thing."

"If you don't believe in marriage, then what do you believe in?"

"Passion," he said. "For as long as it burns hot. But that's it."

She nodded slowly, and then she turned away from him.

"Aren't you going to ride?"

"I… Not right now. I need to… I need to go think."

And then without another word, Emerson Maxfield ran away from him.

The cabin was a shit hole. He really wasn't enjoying staying there. He had worked himself out of places like this. Marginal dwellings that had only woodstoves for heat. But this was the situation. Revenge was a dish best served cold, and apparently his ass had to be kind of cold right along with it.

Not that he didn't know how to build a fire. It seemed tonight he'd have to.

He went outside, into the failing light, wearing nothing but his jeans and a pair of boots, and searched around for an ax.

There was no preprepared firewood. That would've been way too convenient, and Holden had the notion that James Maxfield was an asshole in just about every way. It wasn't just Soraya that James didn't care about. It was everyone. Right down to the people who lived and worked on his property. He didn't much care about the convenience of his employees. It was a good reminder. Of why Holden was here.

Though, Emerson seemed to be under the impression that James cared for *her*. An interesting thing. Because when she had spoken about trying to earn the approval of one of her parents, he had been convinced, of course, that she had meant James's.

But apparently, James was proud of his daughter, and supported her.

Maybe James had used up every ounce of his humanity in his parenting. Though, Holden still had questions about that.

And it was also entirely possible that Emerson knew the truth about how her father behaved. And that she was complicit in covering up his actions in order to protect the brand.

Holden didn't know, and he didn't care. He couldn't concern himself with the fate of anyone involved with James Maxfield.

If you drink water from a poison well, whatever happened, happened.

As far as Holden was concerned, each and every grapevine on this property was soaked through with James Maxfield's poison.

He found an ax and swung it up in the air, splitting the log in front of him with ease. That, at least, did something to get his body warmed up, and quell some of the murder in his blood. He chuckled, positioned another log on top of the large stone sitting before him and swung the ax down.

"Well," came the sound of a soft, feminine voice. "I didn't expect to find you out here. Undressed."

He paused, and turned to see Emerson standing there, wearing a belted black coat, her dark hair loose.

She was wearing high heels.

Nothing covered her legs.

It was cold, and she was standing out in the middle of the muddy ground in front of his cabin, and none of it made much sense.

"What the hell are you doing here?" He looked her up and down. "Dressed like that."

"I could ask you the same question. Why didn't you put a shirt on? It's freezing out here."

"Why didn't *you* put pants on?"

She hesitated, but only for a moment, and then her expression went regal, which he was beginning to recognize meant she was digging deep to find all her stubbornness.

"Because I would be burdened by having to take them off again soon. At least, that's what I hope." Only the faint pink color in her cheeks betrayed the fact that she'd embarrassed herself. Otherwise he'd have thought she was nothing more than an ice queen, throwing out the suggestion of a seduction so cold it might give his dick frostbite.

But that wasn't the truth. No, he could see it in that blush. Underneath all that coolness, Emerson was burning.

And damned if he wasn't on fire himself.

But it made no damn sense to him, that this woman, the princess of Maxfield Vineyards, would come all the way out here, dragging her designer heels in the mud, to seduce him.

He looked behind his shoulder at the tiny cabin, then back at her.

"Really," he said.

The color in her cheeks deepened.

Lust and interest fired through him, and damned if he'd do anything to stop it. Dark, tempting images of taking Emerson into that rough cabin and sullying her on the rock-hard mattress… It was satisfying on so many levels, he couldn't even begin to sort through them all.

His enemy's daughter. Naked and begging for him, in a cabin reserved for workers, people James clearly thought so far beneath his own family that he'd not even given a thought to their basic needs.

Knowing Holden could have her in there, in a hundred different ways, fired his blood in a way nothing but rage had for ages.

Damn, he was hungry for her. In this twisted, intense way he had told himself he wasn't going to indulge.

But she was here.

Maybe with nothing on under that coat. Which meant they were both already half undressed, and it begged the question whether or not they should go ahead and get naked the rest of the way.

A look at her hand. He noticed she didn't have her engagement ring on.

"What the hell kind of game are you playing?" he asked.

"You said that whatever happened between you and a woman in bed was between you and that woman. Well, I'm of the same mind. It's nobody's business but ours what happens here." She bit her lip. "I'm going to be really, really honest with you."

There was something about that statement that burned, because if there was one thing he was never going to be with her, it was honest.

"I don't love my fiancé. I haven't slept with him. Why? Because I'm not that interested in sleeping with him. It's the strangest thing. We've been together for a couple of years, but we don't live near each other. And every time we could have, we just didn't. And the fact that we're not even tempted… Well, that tells you something about the chemistry between us. But this…you. I want to do this with you. It's all I can think about, and trust me when I say that's not me. I don't understand it, I didn't ask for it, or want it, but I can't fight it."

"I'm supposed to be flattered that you're deigning to come down from your shining tower because you can't stop thinking about me?"

"I want you," she said, lifting her chin up. "You asked me earlier if there was anything I had ever wanted that I couldn't have. It's you. I shouldn't have you. But I want you. And if my father found out that I was doing this, he would kill us both. Because my engagement to Donovan matters to him."

"You said you had an arrangement," he stated.

"Oh, Donovan wouldn't care. Donovan knows. I mean, in a vague sense. I texted him to make sure I wasn't just making assumptions. And I found out he already has. Been with someone else, I mean. So, it's not a big deal. But my father… He would never want it being made public. Image is everything to him, and my engagement to Donovan is part of the image right now."

And just like that, he sensed that her relationship with her father was a whole lot more complicated than she let on. But her relationship with James wasn't Holden's problem either way. And neither was whether or not Emerson was a good person, or one who covered up her father's transgressions. None of it mattered.

Nothing really mattered right here but the two of them.

The really fascinating thing was, Emerson didn't know who Holden was. And even if she did, she didn't need anything from him. Not monetarily. It had been a long damn time since he'd appealed to a woman in a strictly physical way. Not that women didn't enjoy him physically. But they also enjoyed what he had—a luxury hotel suite, connections, invitations to coveted parties.

He was standing here with none of that, nothing but a very dilapidated cabin that wasn't even his own.

And she wanted him.

And that, he found, was an incredibly compelling aphrodisiac, a turn-on he hadn't even been aware he'd been missing.

Emerson had *no idea* that he was Holden McCall, the wealthiest developer in the state. All she wanted was a roll in the hay, and why the hell not? Sure, he was supposed to hate her and everything she stood for.

But there was something to be said for a hate screw.

"So let me get this straight," he said. "You haven't even kissed me. You don't even know if I want to kiss you. But you were willing to come down here not even knowing what the payoff would be?"

Her face was frozen, its beauty profound even as she stared at him with blank blue eyes, her red lips pressed into a thin line. And he realized, this was not a woman who knew how to endure being questioned.

She was a woman used to getting what she wanted. A woman used to commanding the show, that much was clear. It was obvious that Emerson was accustomed to bulldozing down doors, a characteristic that seemed to stand in sharp contrast to the fact that she also held deep concerns over what her parents thought of her and her decisions.

"That should tell you, then," she said, the words stiff. "It should tell you how strong I think the connection is. If it's not as strong for you, that's fine. You're not the one on the verge of getting married, and you're just a man, after all. So you'll get yours either way. This might be *it* for me before I go to the land of boring, banal monogamous sex."

"So you intend to be fully faithful to this man you're marrying? The one you've never been naked with?"

"What's the point of marriage otherwise? You said that yourself. I believe in monogamy. It's just in my particular style of engagement I feel a little less… intense about it than I otherwise might."

He could take this moment to tell her that her father certainly didn't seem to look at marriage that way. But that would be stupid. He didn't have enough information yet to come at James, and when he did, he wasn't going to miss.

"So you just expect that I'll fuck you whether I feel a connection to you or not. Even if I don't feel like it."

She lifted her chin, her imperiousness seeming to intensify. "It's my understanding that men always feel like it."

"Fair enough," he said. "But that's an awfully low bar, don't you think?"

"I don't…"

"I'll tell you what," he said. "I'm going to give you a kiss. And if afterward you can walk away, then you should."

She blinked. "I don't want to."

"See how you feel after the kiss."

He dropped the ax, and it hit the frozen ground with a dull thump.

He already knew.

He already knew that he was going to have a hard time getting his hands off her once they'd been on her. The way that she appealed to him hit a primitive part of him he couldn't explain. A part of him that was something other than civilized.

She took a step toward him, those ridiculous high heels somehow skimming over the top of the dirt and rocks. She was soft and elegant, and he was half dressed and sweaty from chopping wood, his breath a cloud in the cold air.

She reached out and put her hand on his chest. And it took every last ounce of his willpower not to grab her wrist and pin her palm to him. To hold her against him, make her feel the way his heart was beginning to rage out of control.

He couldn't remember the last time he'd wanted a woman like this.

And he didn't know if it was the touch of the forbidden adding to the thrill, or if it was the fact that she wanted his body and nothing else. Because he could do nothing for Emerson Maxfield, not Holden Brown, the man he was pretending to be. The man who had to depend on the good graces of his employer and lived in a cabin on the property. There was nothing he could do for her.

Nothing he could do but make her scream his name, over and over again.

And that was all she wanted.

She was a woman set to marry another man. She didn't even want emotions from him.

She wanted nothing. Nothing but his body.

And he couldn't remember the last time that was the case, if ever. Everyone wanted something from him. Everyone wanted a piece of him.

Even his mother and sister, who he cared for dearly, needed him. They needed his money, they needed his support.

They needed him to engage in a battle to destroy the man who had devastated Soraya.

But this woman standing in front of him truly wanted only this elemental thing, this spark of heat between them to become a blaze. And who was he to deny her?

He let her guide it. He let her be the one to make the next move. Here she was, all bold in that coat, with her hand on his chest, and yet there was a hesitancy to her as well. She didn't have a whole lot of experience seducing men, that much was obvious. And damned if he didn't enjoy the moment where she had to steel herself and find the courage to lean in.

There was something so very enjoyable about a woman playing the vixen when it was clear it wasn't her natural role. But she was doing it. For him. All for the desire she felt for him.

What man wouldn't respond to that?

She licked her lips, and then she pressed her mouth to his.

And that was the end of his control.

He wrapped his arm around her waist and pressed her against him, angling his head and consuming her.

Because the fire that erupted between them wasn't something that could be tamed. Wasn't something that could be controlled. Couldn't be tested or tasted. This was not a cocktail to be sipped. He wanted to drink it all down, and her right along with it.

Needed to. There was no other option.

He felt like a dying man making a last gasp for breath in the arms of this woman he should never have touched.

He didn't let his hands roam over her curves, no matter how much he wanted to. He simply held her, licking his way into the kiss, his tongue sliding against hers as he tasted the most luscious forbidden fruit that had ever been placed in front of him.

But it wasn't enough to have a bite. He wanted her juices to run down his chin. And he was going to have just that.

"Want to walk away?" he asked, his voice rough, his body hard.

"No," she breathed.

And then he lifted her up and carried her into the cabin.

Five

If this moment were to be translated into a head-line, it would read: Maxfield Heiress Sacrifices All for an Orgasm.

Assuming, of course, that she would have an or-gasm. She'd never had one yet with a man. But if she were going to…it would be with him.

If it were possible, it would be now.

When she had come up to the cabin and seen him standing there chopping wood—of all things—his chest bare, his jeans slung low on his hips, she had known that all good sense and morality were lost. Utterly and completely lost. In a fog of lust that showed no sign of lifting.

There was nothing she could do but give in.

Because she knew, she absolutely *knew*, that whatever this was needed to be explored. That she could not marry Donovan wondering what this thing between herself and Holden was.

Not because she thought there might be something lasting between them—no—she was fairly certain this was one of those moments of insanity that had nothing to do with anything like real life or good sense.

But she needed to know what desire was. Needed to know what sex could be.

For all she knew, this was the key to unlocking it with the man she was going to marry. And that was somewhat important. Maybe Holden was her particular key.

The man who was destined to teach her about her own sexuality.

Whatever the excuse, she was in his arms now, being carried into a modest cabin that was a bit more run-down than she had imagined any building on the property might be.

She had never been in any of the workers' quarters before. She had never had occasion to.

She shivered, with cold or fear she didn't know.

This was like some strange, unexpected, delayed rebellion. Sneaking out of her room in the big house to come and fool around with one of the men who worked for her father. He would be furious if he knew.

And so he would never know.

No one would ever know about this. No one but the two of them.

It would be their dirty secret. And at the moment, she was hoping that it would be very, very dirty. Because she had never had these feelings in her life.

This desire to get naked as quickly as possible. To be as close to someone as possible.

She wanted to get this coat off and rub herself all over his body, and she had never, ever felt that before.

She was a woman who was used to being certain. She knew why she made the decisions she did, and she made them without overthinking.

She was *confident*.

But this was a part of herself she had never been terribly confident in.

Oh, it had nothing to do with her looks. Men liked her curves. She knew that. She didn't have insecurities when it came to her body.

It was what her body was capable of. What it could feel.

That gave her all kinds of insecurity. Enough that in her previous relationships she had decided to make her own pleasure a nonissue. If ever her college boyfriend had noticed that she hadn't climaxed, he had never said. But he had been young enough, inexperienced enough, that he might not have realized.

She was sure, however, that her last ex had realized.

Occasionally he'd asked her if she was all right. And she had gotten very good at soothing his ego.

It's nice to be close.

It was good for me.

And one night, when he had expressed frustration at her tepid response to his kisses, she had simply shrugged and said, *I'm not very sexual.*

And she had believed it. She had believed each and every one of those excuses. And had justified the times when she had faked it, because of course her inability to feel something wasn't his fault.

But just looking at Holden made a pulse pound between her thighs that was more powerful than any sensation she'd felt during intercourse with a man before.

And with his hands on her like they were right now, with her body cradled in his strong arms...

She could barely breathe. She could barely think.

All she felt was a blinding, white-hot shock of need, and she had never experienced anything like it before in her life.

He set her down on the uneven wood floor. It was cold.

"I was going to build a fire," he said. "Wait right here, I'll be back."

And then he went back outside, leaving her standing in the middle of the cabin, alone and not in his arms, which gave her a moment to pause.

Was she really about to do this?

She didn't have any experience with casual sex. She had experience with sex only in the context of a relationship. And she had never, ever felt anything this intense.

It was the intensity that scared her. Not so much the fact that it was physical only, but the fact that it was so incredibly physical.

She didn't know how this might change her.

Because she absolutely felt like she was on the cusp of being changed. And maybe that was dramatic, but she couldn't rid herself of the sensation. This was somehow significant. It would somehow alter the fabric of who she was. She felt brittle and thin, on the verge of being shattered. And she wasn't entirely sure what was going to put her back together.

It was frightening, that thought. But not frightening enough to make her leave.

He returned a moment later, a stack of wood in his arms.

And she watched as he knelt down before the woodstove, his muscles shifting and bunching in his back as he began to work at lighting a fire.

"I didn't realize the cabins were so…rustic."

"They are a bit. Giving you second thoughts?"

"No," she said quickly.

If he changed his mind now, if he sent her away, she would die. She was sure of it.

He was kneeling down half naked, and he looked so damned hot that he chased away the cold.

"It'll take a bit for the fire to warm the place up," he said. "But I can keep you warm in the meantime."

He stood, brushing the dust off his jeans and making his way over to her.

She had meant to—at some point—take stock of the room. To look around and see what furniture it had, get a sense of the layout. But she found it too hard to look away from him. And when he fixed those eyes on her, she was held captive.

Utterly and completely.

His chest was broad, sprinkled with just the right amount of hair, his muscles cut and well-defined. His pants were low, showing those lines that arrow downward, as if pointing toward the most masculine part of him.

She had never been with a man who had a body like this. It was like having only ever eaten store-bought pie, and suddenly being treated to a home-made extravaganza.

"You are… You're beautiful," she said.

He chuckled. "I think that's my line."

"No. It's definitely mine."

One side of his mouth quirked upward into a grin, and even though the man was a stranger to her, suddenly she felt like he might not be.

Because that smile touched her somewhere inside her chest and made her *feel* when she knew it ought not to. Because this should be about just her body. And not in any way about her heart. But it was far too easy to imagine a world where nothing existed beyond this cabin, beyond this man and the intensity in his eyes, the desire etched into every line of his face.

And that body. Hot *damn*, that body.

Yes, it was very easy to imagine she was a different girl who lived in a different world.

Who could slip away to a secluded cabin and find herself swept up in the arms of a rugged cowboy, and it didn't matter whether or not it was *on brand*. Right now, it didn't.

Right now, it didn't.

This was elemental, something deeper than reality. It was fantasy in all of its bright, brilliant glory. Except it was real. Brought to life with stunning visuals, and it didn't matter whether it should be or not.

It was.

It felt suddenly much bigger than her. And because of that, she felt more connected with her body than she ever had before.

Because this wasn't building inside of her, it surrounded her, encompassed her. She could never have contained so much sensation, so much need. And so it became the world around her.

Until she couldn't remember what it was like to draw breath in a space where his scent didn't fill her lungs, where her need didn't dictate the way she stood, the way she moved.

She put her hands on the tie around her waist.

And he watched.

His attention was rapt, his focus unwavering.

The need between her thighs escalated.

She unknotted the belt and then undid the buttons, let her coat fall to her feet.

She was wearing nothing but a red lace bra and panties and her black high heels.

"Oh, Little Red," he growled. "I do like that color on you."

The hunger in his eyes was so intense she could feel it echoing inside of herself. Could feel her own desire answering back.

No man had ever looked at her like this.

They had wanted her, sure. Had desired her.

But they hadn't wanted to consume her, and she had a feeling that her own personal Big Bad Wolf just might.

She expected him to move to her, but instead he moved away, walking over to the bed that sat in the corner of the humble room. He sat on the edge of the mattress, his thighs splayed, his eyes fixed on her.

"I want you to come on over here," he said.

She began to walk toward him, her heels clicking on the floor, and she didn't need to be given detailed instruction, because she somehow knew what he wanted.

It was strange, and it was impossible, that somehow this man she had barely spent any time with felt known to her in a way that men she'd dated for long periods of time never had.

But he did.

And maybe that was something she had overlooked in all of this.

What she wanted to happen between them might be physical, but there was a spiritual element that couldn't be denied. Something that went deeper than just attraction. Something that spoke to a more desperate need.

His body was both deliciously unknown, and somehow right and familiar all at the same time.

And so were his needs.

She crossed the room and draped an arm over his shoulder, lifting her knee to the edge of the mattress, rocking forward so that the center of her pressed against his hardness. "I'm here," she said.

He wrapped his arm around her waist, pushed his fingertips beneath the waistband of her panties and slid his hands down over her ass. Then he squeezed. Hard. And she gasped.

"I'm going to go out on a limb here and guess that part of the attraction you have to all of this is that it's a little bit rough."

She licked her lips, nodded when no words would come.

She hadn't realized that was what she'd wanted, but when he said it, it made sense. When he touched her like this—possessive and commanding—she knew it was what she needed.

"That suits me just fine, princess, because I'm a man who likes it that way. So you have to tell me right now if you can handle it."

"I can handle whatever you give me," she said, her voice coming out with much more certainty than she felt.

Rough.

The word skated over her skin, painted delicious pictures in her mind and made that place between her legs throb with desire.

Rough. Uncivilized. Untamed.

Right then she wanted that, with a desperation that defied explanation.

She wanted to be marked by this. Changed by it. She wanted to have the evidence of it on her skin as well as on her soul.

Because somehow she felt that tonight, in this bed, it might be the only chance she'd have to find out what she was.

What she wanted.

What she desired apart from anything else, apart from family and social expectations. Tonight, this, had nothing to do with what anyone else might expect of her.

This was about her.

And on some level she felt like if she didn't have this, the rest of her life would be a slow descent into the madness of wondering.

"If anything goes too far for you, you just say it, you understand?"

"Yes," she said.

"I want to make you scream," he said. "But I want it to be the good kind."

She had never in her life screamed during sex.

The promise, the heat in his eyes, made her suspect she was about to.

That was when he tightened his grip on her and reversed their positions.

He pinned her down on her back, grabbing both wrists with one hand and stretching her arms up over her head. He had his thighs on either side of her hips, the denim rough against her skin. He was large and hard and glorious above her, his face filled with the kind of intensity that thrilled her down to her core.

She rocked her hips upward, desperate for fulfillment. Desperate to be touched by him.

He denied her.

He held her pinned down and began a leisurely tour of her body with his free hand.

He traced her collarbone, the edge of her bra, down the valley between her breasts and to her belly button. Before tracing the edge of her panties. But he didn't touch her anywhere that she burned for him. And she could feel the need for his touch, as if those parts of her were lit up bright with their demand for him. And still, he wouldn't do it.

"I thought you said this was going to be rough."

"Rough's not fun if you're not good and wet first," he said. And then he leaned in, his lips right next to her ear. "And I'm going to make sure you get really, really wet first."

Just those words alone did the job. An arrow of need pierced her center, and she could feel it, molten liquid there in her thighs. And that was when he captured her mouth with his, kissing her deep and long, cupping her breast with one hand and teasing her nipple with his thumb.

She whimpered, arching her hips upward, frustrated when there was nothing there for her to make contact with.

He touched her slowly, thoroughly, first through the lace of her bra, before pushing the flimsy fabric down and exposing her breasts. He touched her bare, his thumbs calloused as they moved over her body.

And then he replaced them with his mouth.

He sucked deep, and she worked her hips against nothing, desperate for some kind of relief that she couldn't find as he tormented her.

She would have said that her breasts weren't sensitive.

But he was proving otherwise.

He scraped his teeth across her sensitive skin. And then he bit down.

She cried out, her orgasm shocking her, filling her cheeks with embarrassed heat as wave after wave of desire pulsed through her core.

But she didn't feel satisfied, because he still hadn't touched her there.

She felt aching and raw, empty when she needed to be filled.

"There's a good girl," he said, and her internal muscles pulsed again.

He tugged her panties down her thighs, stopping at her ankles before pushing her knees wide, eyeing her hungrily as he did.

Then he leaned in, inhaling her scent, pressing a kiss to the tender skin on her leg. "The better to eat you with," he said, looking her in the eye as he lowered his head and dragged his tongue through her slick folds.

She gasped. This was the first time he had touched her there, and it was so… So impossibly dirty. So impossibly intimate.

Then he was done teasing. Done talking. He grabbed her hips and pulled her forward, his grip bruising as he set his full focus and attention on consuming her.

She dug her heels into the bed, tried to brace herself, but she couldn't. She had no control over this, over any of it.

He was driving her toward pleasure at his pace, and it was terrifying and exhilarating all at once.

She climaxed again. Impossibly.

It was then she realized he was no longer holding her in place, but she had left her own wrists up above her head, as if she were still pinned there.

She was panting, gasping for breath, when he moved up her body, his lips pressing against hers.

She could taste her own desire there, and it made her shiver.

"Now I want you to turn over," he said.

She didn't even think of disobeying that commanding voice. She did exactly as she was told.

"Up on your knees, princess," he said.

She obeyed, anticipation making the base of her spine tingle as she waited.

She could hear plastic tearing, knew that he must be getting naked. Getting a condom on.

And when he returned to her, he put one hand on her hip, and she felt the head of his arousal pressed against the entrance to her body.

She bit her lip as he pushed forward, filling her.

He was so big, and this was not a position she was used to.

It hurt a bit as he drove his hips forward, a short curse escaping his lips as he sank in to the hilt.

She lowered her head, and he placed his hand between her shoulder blades, drawing it down her spine, then back up. And she wanted to purr like a very contented cat. Then he grabbed hold of both her hips, pulling out slowly, and slamming back home.

She gasped, arching her back as she met him thrust for punishing thrust. She pressed her face down into the mattress as he entered her, over and over again, the only sounds in the room that of skin meeting skin, harsh breaths and the kinds of feral sounds she had never imagined could come from her.

He grabbed hold of her hair, and moved it to one side, and she felt a slight tug, and then with a pull that shocked her with its intensity, he lifted her head as he held her like that, the tug matching his thrust. She gasped, the pain on her scalp somehow adding to the pleasure she felt between her legs.

And he did it over and over again.

Until she was sobbing. Until she was begging for release.

Then he released his hold on her hair, grabbing both her hips again as he raced her to the end, his hold on her bruising, his thrusts pushing her to the point of pain. Then he leaned forward, growling low and biting her neck as he came hard. And she followed him right over the edge into oblivion.

Six

By the time Emerson went limp in front of him, draped over the mattress like a boneless cat, the fire had begun to warm the space.

Holden was a man who didn't have much in the way of regret in his life—it was impossible when he had been raised with absolutely nothing, and had gotten to a space where he didn't have to worry about his own basic needs, or those of his family. And even now, it was difficult to feel anything but the kind of bone-deep satisfaction that overtook him.

He went into the bathroom and took care of the practicalities, then went back to stoke the fire.

He heard the sound of shifting covers on the bed, and looked over his shoulder to see Emerson lying on her side now, her legs crossed just so, hiding that tempting shadow at the apex of her thighs, her arm draped coquettishly over her breast.

"Enjoying the show?" he asked.

"Yes," she responded, no shame in her voice at all.

"You might return the favor," he said.

She looked down at her own body, as if she only just realized that she was covering a good amount of the tempting bits.

"You're busy," she said. "Making a fire. I would hate to distract."

"You're distracting even as you are."

Maybe even especially as she was, looking timid when he knew how she really was. Wild and uninhibited and the best damn sex he'd ever had in his life.

Hard mattress notwithstanding.

She rolled onto her back then, stretching, raising her arms up above her head, pointing her toes.

He finished with the fire quickly, and returned to the bed.

"I couldn't do it again," she said, her eyes wide.

"Why not?"

"I've never come that many times in a row in my life. Surely it would kill you."

"I'm willing to take the chance," he said.

It surprised him to hear that her response wasn't normal for her. She had seemed more than into it. Though, she had talked about the tepid chemistry between herself and the man she was engaged to.

There was something wrong with that man, because if he couldn't find chemistry with Emerson, Holden doubted he could find it with anyone.

"Well, of course you're willing to take the chance. You're not the one at risk. You only... Once. I already did three times."

"Which means you have the capacity for more," he said. "At least, that's my professional opinion."

"Professional ranch hand opinion? I didn't know that made you an expert on sex."

He chuckled. "I'm an expert on sex because of vast experience in my personal life, not my professional life. Though, I can tell you I've never considered myself a hobbyist when it came to female pleasure. Definitely a professional."

"Well, then I guess I picked a good man to experiment with."

"Is that what this is? An experiment?"

She rolled over so she was halfway on his body, her breast pressed against his chest, her blue eyes suddenly sincere. "I've never had an orgasm with a man before. I have them on my own. But never with... Never with a partner. I've only been with two men. But... They were my boyfriends. So you would think that if it was this easy they would have figured it out. Or I would have figured it out. And I can't for the life of me figure out why we didn't. Myself included."

"Chemistry," he said, brushing her hair back from her face, surprising himself with the tender gesture. But now she was asking him these wide-eyed innocent questions, when she had done things with him only moments ago that were anything but.

"Chemistry," she said. "I thought it might be something like that. Something magical and strange and completely impossible to re-create in a lab setting, sadly."

"We can re-create it right now."

"But what if I can't ever re-create it again? Although, I suppose now I know that it's possible for me to feel this way, I…"

"I didn't know that I was your one-man sexual revolution."

"Well, I didn't want to put that kind of pressure on you."

"I thrive under pressure."

It was easy to forget, right now, that she was the daughter of his enemy. That he was here to destroy her family. That her engagement and the lack of chemistry between herself and her fiancé would be the least of her worries in the next week.

In fact, maybe he could spare her from the marriage. Because the optics for the family would be pretty damned reduced, probably beyond the point of healing. Her marriage to an ad exec was hardly going to fix that.

And anyway, the man would probably be much less interested in marrying into the Maxfield dynasty when it was reduced to more of a one-horse outfit and they didn't have two coins to rub together.

Holden waited for there to be guilt. But he didn't feel it.

Instead, he felt some kind of indefinable sense of satisfaction. Like in the past few moments he had collected another chess piece that had once belonged to his enemy. And Emerson was so much more than a pawn.

But he didn't know how to play this victory. Not yet.

And anyway, she didn't feel much like a victory or a conquest lying here in bed with him when he was still naked. He felt more than a little bit conquered himself.

"This is terrifying," she whispered. "Because I shouldn't be here. And I shouldn't be with you at all. And I think this is the most relaxed and maybe even the happiest I've ever felt in my life." She looked up at him, and a tear tracked down her cheek, and just like that, the guilt hit him right in the chest. "And I know that it can't go beyond tonight. I know it can't. Because you have your life... And I have mine."

"And there's no chance those two things could ever cross," he said, the words coming out a hell of a lot more hostile than he intended.

"I'm not trying to be snobby or anything," she said. "But there's expectations about the kind of man that I'll end up with. And what he'll bring to the family."

"Princess, I don't know why you're talking about marriage."

"Well, that's another problem in and of itself, isn't it? I'm at that point. Where marriage has to be considered."

"You're at that point? What the hell does that mean? Are we in the 1800s?"

"In a family like mine, it matters. We have to… My father doesn't have sons. His daughters have to marry well, marry men who respect and uphold the winery. His sons-in-law are going to gain a certain amount of ownership of the place, and that means…"

"His sons-in-law are getting ownership of the business?"

"Yes," she said. "I mean, I'll retain my share as well, so don't think it's that kind of draconian nonsense. But when we marry, Donovan is going to get a share of the winery. As large as mine. When Wren marries, it will be the same. Then there's Cricket, and her husband will get a share as well, though not as large. And by the time that's all finished, my father will only have a portion. A very small portion."

"How does that math work? Cricket gets less?"

"Well, so far Cricket doesn't have any interest in running the place, and she never has. So yes."

"No wonder your father is so invested in controlling who you marry."

"It's for my protection as well. It's not like he wants me getting involved with fortune hunters."

"You really are from another world," he said, disdain in his voice, even though he didn't mean it to be there. Because it didn't matter. Because it wasn't true—he had money, he had status. And because he didn't care about her. Or her opinion. He didn't care that she was as shallow as the rest of her family, as her father. It didn't concern him and, in fact, was sort of helpful given the fact that he had taken pretty terrible advantage of her, that he'd lied to her to get her into bed.

"I can tell that you think I'm a snob," she said. "I'm not, I promise. I wouldn't get naked with a man I thought was beneath me."

"Well, that's BS. It's a pretty well-documented fact that people find slumming to be titillating, Emerson."

"Well, I don't. You're different. And yes, I find that sexy. You're forbidden, and maybe I find that sexy too, but it's not about you being less than me, or less than other men that I've been with. Somehow, you're more, and I don't know what to do with that. That's why it hurts. Because I don't know if I will ever feel as contented, ever again, as I do right now lying in this cabin, and this is not supposed to be…"

"It's not supposed to be anything you aspire to. How could it be? When your mother thinks that what you have is beneath you as it is."

She swallowed and looked away. "My life's not mine. It's attached to this thing my father built from scratch. This legacy that has meant a life that I'm grateful for, whatever you might think. I don't need to have gone without to understand that what I've been given is extraordinary. I do understand that.

But it's an incredible responsibility to bear as well, and I have to be…a steward of it. Whether I want to be or not."

And suddenly, he resented it all. Every last bit. The lies that stood between them, the way she saw him, and his perceived lack of power in this moment. He growled, reversing their positions so he was over her.

"None of that matters just now," he said.

She looked up at him, and then she touched his face. "No," she agreed. "I don't suppose it does."

He reached down and found her red lace bra, touching the flimsy fabric and then looking back at her. He took hold of her wrists, like he'd done earlier, and, this time, secured them tightly with the lace.

"Right now, you're here," he said. "And I'm the only thing you need to worry about. You're mine right here, and there's nothing outside this room, off of this bed, do you understand?"

Her breath quickened, her breasts rising and falling with the motion. She nodded slowly.

"Good girl," he said. "You have a lot of responsibilities outside, but when you're here, the only thing you have to worry about is pleasing me."

This burned away the words of the last few minutes, somehow making it all feel okay again, even if it shouldn't. As if securing her wrists now might help him hold on to this moment a little tighter. Before he had to worry about the rest, before he had to deal with the fallout and what it would mean for Emerson.

This thing that she cared about so deeply, this dynasty, which she was willing to marry a man she didn't care about at all to secure.

He would free her from it, and in the end, it might be a blessing.

He looked at the way her wrists were tied, and suddenly he didn't want to free her at all.

What he wanted was to keep her.

He got a condom from his wallet and returned to her, where she lay on the bed, her wrists bound, her thighs spread wide in invitation.

He sheathed himself and gripped her hips, entering her in one smooth stroke. Her climax was instant, and it was hard, squeezing him tight as he pounded into her without mercy.

And he set about proving to her that there was no limit to the number of times she could find her pleasure.

But there was a cost to that game, one that crystallized in his mind after the third time she cried out his name and settled herself against his chest, her wrists still tightly tied.

She was bound to him now.

And she had betrayed a very crucial piece of information.

And the ways it could all come together for him became suddenly clear.

He knew exactly what he was going to do.

Seven

It had been three days since her night in the cabin with Holden. And he was all she could think about. She knew she was being ridiculous. They had another event happening at the winery tonight, and she couldn't afford to be distracted.

There was going to be an engagement party in the large barn, which had been completely and totally made over into an elegant, rustic setting, with vast open windows that made the most of the view, and elegant chandeliers throughout.

Tonight's event wasn't all on her shoulders. Mostly, it was Wren's responsibility, but Emerson was helping, and she had a feeling that in her current state she wasn't helping much.

All she could do was think about Holden. The

things he had done to her body. The things he had taught her about her body.

She felt like an idiot. Spinning fantasies about a man, obsessing about him.

She'd never realized she would be into something like bondage, but he had shown her the absolute freedom there could be in giving up control.

She was so used to controlling everything all the time. And for just a few hours in his bed, he had taken the lead. It was like a burden had been lifted from her.

"Are you there, Emerson? It's me, Wren."

Emerson turned to look at her sister, who was fussing with the guest list in front of her.

"I'm here, and I've been here, helping you obsess over details."

"You're here," Wren said. "But you're not *here*."

Emerson looked down at her left hand and cursed. Because there was supposed to be a ring there. She had taken it off before going to Holden's cabin, but she needed to get it back on before tonight. Before she was circulating in a room full of guests.

Tonight's party was different from a brand-related launch. The event was at the heart of the winery itself, and as the manager of the property, Wren was the person taking the lead. When it came to broader brand representation, it was down to Emerson. But Emerson would still be taking discreet photographs of the event to share on social media, as that helped with the broader awareness of the brand.

Their jobs often crossed, as this was a family operation and not a large corporation. But neither of them minded. And in fact, Emerson considered it a good day when she got to spend extra time with her sister. But less so today when Wren was so apparently frazzled.

"What's wrong with you?" Wren asked, and then her eye fell meaningfully to her left hand. "Did something happen with Donovan?"

"No," Emerson said. "I just forgot to put the ring on."

"That doesn't sound like you. Because you're ever conscious of the fact that a ring like that is a statement."

"I'm well aware of what I'm ever conscious of, *Wren*," she said. "I don't need you to remind me."

"And yet, you forgot something today, so it seems like you need a reminder."

"It's really nothing."

"Except it *is* something. Because if it were nothing, then you wouldn't be acting weird."

"Fine. Don't tell anyone," Emerson said, knowing already that she would regret what she was about to say.

"I like secrets," Wren said, leaning in.

"I had a… I had a one-night stand." Her sister stared at her. Unmoving. "With a man."

Wren huffed a laugh. "Well, I didn't figure you were telling me about the furniture in your bedroom."

"I mean, Donovan and I aren't exclusive, but it didn't feel right to wear his ring while I was…with someone else."

"I had no idea," Wren said, her eyes widening. "I didn't know you were that…"

"Much of a hussy?"

"That *progressive*," she said.

"Well, I'm not. In general. But I was, and am a little thrown off by it. And no one can ever know."

"Solemnly swear."

"You cannot tell Cricket."

"Why would I tell Cricket? She would never be able to look you in the eyes again, and she would absolutely give you away. Not on purpose, mind you."

"No, but it's a secret that she couldn't handle."

"Absolutely."

"Have you met a man that you just…couldn't get out of your head even though he was absolutely unsuitable?"

Wren jolted, her whole body looking like it had been touched by a live wire. "I am very busy with my job."

"Wren."

"Yes. Fine. I do know what it's like to have a sexual obsession with the wrong guy. But I've never… acted on it." The look on her face was so horrified it would have been funny, if Emerson herself hadn't just done the thing that so appalled her sister.

"There's nothing wrong with…being with someone you want, is there? No, I don't really know him, but I knew I wanted him and that seems like a decent reason to sleep with someone, right?"

Wren looked twitchy. "I… Look. Lust and like aren't the same. I get it."

"I like him fine enough," Emerson said. "But we can't ever… *He works for Dad.*"

"Like…in the corporate office?"

"No, like, on the ranch."

"Emersonnnnn."

"What?"

"Are you living out a stable boy fantasy?"

Emerson drew her lip between her teeth and worried it back and forth. "He's not a boy. He's a man. On that you can trust me."

"The question stands."

"Maybe it was sort of that fantasy, I don't know. It was a fantasy, that much I can tell you. But it was supposed to just happen and be done, and I'm obsessing about him instead."

"Who would have ever thought that could happen?" Wren asked in mock surprise.

"In this advanced modern era, I should simply be able to claim my sexuality. Own it! Bring it with me wherever I go. Not…leave it behind in some rundown cabin with the hottest man I've ever seen in my life."

"Those are truly sage words. You should put them on a pretty graphic and post it to your page. Hashtag—girl-boss-of-your-own-sexuality. Put your hair up and screw his brains out!"

Emerson shot her sister a deadly glare. "You know I hate that."

"I also know you never put a toe out of line, and yet here you are, confessing an extremely scandalous transgression."

"This secret goes to your grave with you, or I put you in the ground early, do you understand?"

Wren smirked and seemed to stretch a little taller, as if reminding Emerson she'd outgrown her by two inches when she was thirteen. She and Wren definitely looked like sisters—the same dark hair and blue eyes—but Wren wasn't curvy. She was tall and lean, her hair sleek like her build. She'd honed her more athletic figure with Krav Maga, kickboxing and all other manner of relatively violent exercise.

She claimed it was the only reason she hadn't killed Creed Cooper yet.

She also claimed she liked knowing she *could* kill him if the occasion arose at one of the many different venues where they crossed paths.

Her martial arts skills were yet another reason it was hilarious for Emerson to threaten her sister. She'd be pinned to the ground in one second flat. Though, as the older sibling, she'd done her part to emotionally scar her sister to the point that, when she'd outgrown her, she still believed on some level Emerson could destroy her.

"In all seriousness," Wren said, "it does concern me. I mean, that you're marrying Donovan, and you're clearly more into whoever this other guy is."

"Right. Because I'm going to marry one of the men that work here. That would go over like... What's heavier than a lead balloon?"

"Does it matter?"

"What kind of ridiculous question is that? Of course it matters."

"Dad has never shown the slightest bit of interest in who I'm dating or not dating."

"You're not the oldest. I think... I think he figures he'll get me out of the way first. And it isn't a matter of him showing interest in who I'm dating. He directly told me that Donovan was the sort of man that I should associate with. He set me up with him."

"You're just going to marry who Dad tells you to marry?"

"Would you do differently, Wren? Honestly, I'm asking you."

"I don't think I could marry a man that I wasn't even attracted to."

"If Dad told you a certain man met with his approval, if he pushed you in that direction...you wouldn't try to make it work?"

Wren looked away. "I don't know. I guess I might have to try, but if after two years I still wasn't interested physically..."

"Marriage is a partnership. Our bodies will change. And sex drives and attraction will all change too. We need to have something in common. I mean, it makes way more sense to marry a man I have a whole host of things in common with than it does to marry one who I just want to be naked with."

"I didn't suggest you marry the ranch hand. But perhaps there's some middle ground. A man you like to talk to, and a man you want to sleep with."

"Well, I have yet to find a middle ground that would be suitable for Dad."

Anyway, Emerson didn't think that Holden could be called a middle ground. Not really. He was something so much more than that. Much too much of an extreme to be called something as neutral as middle ground.

"Maybe you should wait until you do."

"Or maybe I should just do what feels best," Emerson said. "I mean, maybe my marriage won't be the best of the best. Maybe I can't have everything. But we are really lucky, you and I. Look at this life." She gestured around the barn. "We have so much. I can make do with whatever I don't have."

Wren looked sad. "I don't know. That seems… tragic to me."

"What about you? You said you wanted a man and you haven't done anything about it."

"That's different."

"So, there's a man you want, and you can't be with him."

"I don't even like him," she said.

Emerson felt bowled over by that statement. Because there was only one man Emerson knew who Wren hated. And the idea that Wren might want him…

Well, no wonder Wren could barely even speak of it. She hated Creed Cooper more than anything else on earth. If the two of them ever touched…well, they would create an explosion of one kind or another, and Emerson didn't know how she hadn't realized that before.

Possibly because she had never before experienced the kind of intense clash she had experienced just a few nights ago with Holden.

"You do understand, then," Emerson said. "That there is a difference between wanting and having. And having for a limited time." She looked down. "Yes, I'm wildly attracted to this guy, and our chemistry is amazing. But it could never be more than that. Though, as someone who has experienced the temporary fun… You know you could."

Wren affected a full-body shudder.

"I really couldn't. I really, really couldn't."

"Suit yourself. But I'm going to go ahead and say that you're not allowed to give me advice anymore, because you live in a big glass house."

"I do not. It's totally different. I'm not marrying someone I shouldn't."

"Well, I'm marrying someone Dad wants me to. I trust Dad. And at the end of the day, I guess that's it. I'm trusting that it's going to be okay because it's what Dad wants me to do, and he's never… He's never steered me wrong. He's never hurt me. All he's ever done is support me."

Her father wanted the best for her. And she knew

it. She was just going to have to trust that in the end, like she trusted him.

"I know," Wren said, putting her arm around Emerson. "At least you have some good memories now."

Emerson smiled. "Really good."

"I don't want details," Wren said, patting Emerson's shoulder.

She flashed back to being tied up in bed with Holden. "I am not giving you details. Those are sacred."

"As long as we're on the same page."

Emerson smiled and went back to the checklist she was supposed to be dealing with. "We are on the same page. Which is currently a checklist. Tonight's party will go off without a hitch."

"Don't jinx it," Wren said, knocking resolutely on one of the wooden tables.

"I'm not going to jinx it. It's one of your parties. So you know it's going to be absolutely perfect."

Eight

The party was going off without a hitch.

Everyone was enjoying themselves, and Emerson was in visual heaven, finding any number of photo opportunities buried in the meticulous decorations that Wren had arranged. With the permission of the couple, she would even share photographs of them, and of the guests. This, at least, served to distract her mildly from the situation with Holden.

Except, there was no *situation*, that was the thing. But it was very difficult for her brain to let go of that truth.

She wanted there to be a situation. But like she had said to Wren earlier, there was really no point in entertaining that idea at all. Marriage was more than just the marriage bed.

And she and Holden might be compatible between the sheets—they were so compatible it made her pulse with desire even thinking about it—but that didn't mean they would be able to make a *relationship*, much less a *marriage*.

They had nothing in common.

You're assuming. You don't actually know that.

Well, it was true. She didn't know, but she could certainly look at the circumstances of his life and make some assumptions.

A passing waiter caught her eye, and she reached out to take hold of a glass of champagne. That was when a couple of things happened all at once. And because they happened so quickly, the reality took her longer to untangle than it might have otherwise.

The first thing she noticed was a man so stunning he took her breath away as he walked into the room.

The second realization was that she knew that man. Even though he looked so different in the sleekly cut black tux he had on his fit body that the name her brain wanted to apply to him couldn't seem to stick.

The third thing that happened was her heart dropping into her feet.

And she didn't even know why.

Because Holden had just walked in wearing a tux.

It might have taken a moment for her brain to link all those details up, but it had now.

She just couldn't figure out what it meant.

That he looked like this. That he was here.

He took a glass of champagne from a tray, and scanned the room. He looked different. But also the same.

Because while he might be clothed in an extremely refined fashion, there was still a ruggedness about him.

Something wild and untamed, even though, on a surface level, he blended in with the people around them.

No, not blended in.

He could never blend in.

He was actually dressed much nicer than anyone else here.

That suit was clearly custom, and it looked horrendously expensive. As did his shoes. As did... everything about him. And could he really be the same man she had happened upon shirtless cutting wood the other day? The same man who had tied her up in his run-down little cabin? The same man who had done desperate, dirty things to her?

And then his eyes collided with hers.

And he smiled.

It made her shiver. It made her ache.

But even so, it was a stranger's smile. It was not the man she knew, and she couldn't make sense of that certainty, even to herself. He walked across the room, acknowledging no one except for her.

And she froze. Like a deer being stalked by a mountain lion. Her heart was pounding in her ears, the sound louder now than the din of chatter going on around her.

"Just the woman I was looking for," he said.

Why did he sound different? He'd been confident in their every interaction. Had never seemed remotely cowed by her position or her money. And maybe that was the real thing she was seeing now.

Not a different man, but one who looked in his element rather than out of it.

"What are you doing here? And where did you get that suit?"

"Would you believe my fairy godmother visited?" The dark humor twisted his lips into a wry smile.

"No," she said, her heart pounding more viciously in her temple.

"Then would you believe that a few of the mice that live in the cabin made the suit for me?"

"Even less likely to believe that. You don't seem like a friend of mice."

"Honey, I'm not really a friend of anyone. And I'm real sorry for what I'm about to do. But if you cooperate with me, things are going to go a whole lot better."

She looked around. As if someone other than him might have answers. Of course, no one offered any if they did. "What do you mean?"

"You see, I haven't been completely honest with you."

"What?"

She couldn't make any sense of this. She looked

around the room to see if they were attracting attention, because surely they must be. Because she felt like what was happening between them was shining bright like a beacon on the hill. But somehow they weren't attracting any attention at all.

"Why don't we go outside. I have a meeting with your father in just a few minutes. Unless…unless you are willing to negotiate with me."

"You have a meeting with my father? Negotiate what?"

The thoughts that rolled through her mind sent her into a panic.

He had obviously filmed what had happened between them. He was going to extort money from her family. He was a con man. No *wonder* he didn't want his picture taken.

All those accusations hovered on the edge of her lips, but she couldn't make them. Not here.

"What do you want?" she asked.

He said nothing. The man was a rock in a suit. No more sophisticated than he'd been in jeans. She'd thought he was different, but he wasn't. This was the real man.

And he was harder, darker than the man she'd imagined he'd been.

Funny how dressing up made that clear.

"What do you want?" she asked again.

She refused to move. She felt like the biggest fool on the planet. How had she trusted this man with her body? He was so clearly not who he said, so clearly…

Of course he hadn't actually wanted her. Of course the only man she wanted was actually just playing a game.

"Revenge," he said. "Nothing more. I'm sorry that you're caught in the middle of it."

"Did you film us?" She looked around, trying to see if people had noticed him yet. They still hadn't. "Did you film us together?"

"No," he said. "I'm not posting anything up on the internet, least of all that."

"Are you going to show my father?"

"No," he said, his lip curling. "This isn't about you, Emerson, whether you believe me or not. It isn't. But what I do next is about you. So I need you to come outside with me."

He turned, without waiting to see if she was with him, and walked back out of the barn. Emerson looked around and then darted after his retreating figure.

When they reached the outdoors, it was dim out, just like the first night they had met. And when he turned to face her, she had the most ridiculous flashback.

He had been in jeans then. With that cowboy hat. And here he was now in a tux. But it was that moment that brought the reality of the situation into focus.

This man was the same man she had been seduced by. Or had she seduced him? It didn't even make sense anymore.

"Tell me what's going on." She looked him up and down. "You clearly aren't actually a ranch hand."

"Your father *did* hire me. Legitimately. So, I guess in total honesty, I do work for your father, and I am a ranch hand."

"What else are you? Are you paparazzi?"

He looked appalled by that. "I'm not a bottom-feeder that makes his living on the misfortunes of others."

"Then what are you? Why are you here?"

"I came here to destroy the winery."

She drew back. The venom in his voice was so intense she could feel the poison sinking down beneath her skin.

He looked her up and down. "But whether or not I do that is up to you now."

"What the hell are you talking about?"

"Your father. Your father had an affair with my sister."

"Your sister? I don't… My father did not have an affair. My father and mother have been married for…more than thirty years. And your sister would have to be…"

"She's younger than you," Holden said. "Younger than you, and incredibly naive about the ways of the world. And your father took advantage of her. When she got pregnant, he tried to pay her to get an abortion, and when she wouldn't, he left. She miscarried, and she's had nothing but health problems since.

"FAST FIVE" READER SURVEY

Your participation entitles you to:

✳ **4 Thank-You Gifts Worth Over \$20!**

Complete the survey in minutes.

Get **2 FREE** Books

See inside for details.

Dear Reader,

Since you are a lover of our books, your opinions are important to us... and so is your time.

That's why we made sure your **"FAST FIVE" READER SURVEY** can be completed in just a few minutes. Your answers to the five questions will help us remain at the forefront of women's fiction.

And, as a thank-you for participating, we'd like to send you **4 FREE THANK-YOU GIFTS!**

Enjoy your gifts with our appreciation,

Pam Powers

To get your
4 FREE THANK-YOU GIFTS:

✴ Quickly complete the "Fast Five" Reader Survey
and return the insert.

"FAST FIVE" READER SURVEY

1 Do you sometimes read a book a second or third time? ○ Yes ○ No

2 Do you often choose reading over other forms of entertainment such as television? ○ Yes ○ No

3 When you were a child, did someone regularly read aloud to you? ○ Yes ○ No

4 Do you sometimes take a book with you when you travel outside the home? ○ Yes ○ No

5 In addition to books, do you regularly read newspapers and magazines? ○ Yes ○ No

YES! I have completed the above Reader Survey. Please send me my 4 FREE GIFTS (gifts worth over $20 retail). I understand that I am under no obligation to buy anything, as explained on the back of this card.

225/326 HDL GNQC

FIRST NAME	LAST NAME

ADDRESS

APT.#	CITY

STATE/PROV.   ZIP/POSTAL CODE

READER SERVICE—Here's how it works:

She's attempted suicide twice and had to be hospitalized. Your father ruined her. Absolutely ruined her."

"No," Emerson said. "It's a mistake. My father would never do that. He would never hurt…"

"I'm not here to argue semantics with you. You can come with me. I'm about to have a meeting with your father, though he doesn't know why. He'll tell you the whole story."

"What does this have to do with me?"

"It didn't have anything to do with you. Until you came to the cabin the other day. I was happy to leave you alone, but you pursued it, and then… And then you told me something very interesting. About the winery. And who'd own it."

Emerson felt like she might pass out. "The man I marry."

"Exactly." He looked at her, those dark eyes blazing. "So you have two choices, really. Let me have that meeting with your father, and you're welcome to attend, where I'll be explaining to him how I've found stacks of NDAs in his employee files. And it doesn't take a genius to figure out why."

"What?"

"Your father has engaged in many, many affairs with workers here on the property. Once I got ahold of the paperwork in his office, I got in touch with some of the women. Most of them wouldn't talk, but enough did. Coercion. And so much of the money for your vineyard comes through all of your celebrity endorsements. Can you imagine the commercial fallout if your father is found to be yet another man who abuses his power? Manipulates women into bed?"

"I don't believe you."

"It doesn't matter whether you believe me or not, Emerson. What matters is that I know I can make other people believe me. And when this is over, you won't be able to give Maxfield wines away with a car wash."

"I don't understand what that gives you," she said, horror coursing through her veins. She couldn't even entertain the idea of this being true. But the truth of it wasn't the thing, not now. The issue was what he could do.

"Revenge," he said, his voice low and hard.

"Revenge isn't a very lucrative business."

"I don't need the revenge to pay. But… I won't lie to you, I find the idea of revenge and a payout very compelling. The idea of owning a piece of this place instead of simply destroying it. So tell me, how does it work? Your husband getting a stake in the business."

"I get married, and then I just call the lawyers, and they'll do the legal paperwork."

His expression became decisive. "Then you and I are getting married."

"And if I don't?"

"I'll publicize the story. I will make sure to ruin the brand. However, if I marry you, what I'll have is ownership of the brand. And you and I, with our united stakes, will have a hell of a lot of decision-making power."

"But to what end?"

"I want your father to know that I ended up owning part of this. And what I do after that…that will depend on what he's willing to do. But I want to make sure he has to contend with me for as long as I want. Yes, I could ruin the label. But that would destroy everything that you and your sister have worked so hard for, and I'm not necessarily here to hurt you. But gaining a piece of this… Making sure my sister gets something, making sure your father knows that I'm right there… That has value to me."

"What about Donovan?"

"He's not my problem. But it's your call, Emerson. You can marry Donovan. And inherit the smoldering wreckage that I'll leave behind. Or, you marry me."

"How do I know you're telling the truth?"

"Look up Soraya Jane on your favorite social media site."

"I… Wait. I know who she is. She's… She has millions of followers."

"I know," he said.

"She's your sister."

"Yes."

"And…"

"My name is Holden. Holden McCall. I am not famous on the internet, or really anywhere. But I'm one of the wealthiest developers in the state. With my money, my sister gained some connections, got into modeling. Started traveling."

"She's built an empire online," Emerson said.

"I know," he said. "What she's done is nothing short of incredible. But she's lost herself. Your father devastated her. Destroyed her. And I can't let that stand."

"So I… If I don't marry you…you destroy everything. And the reason for me marrying Donovan doesn't even exist anymore."

"That's the size of it."

"And we have to transfer everything before my father realizes what you're doing."

Emerson had no idea what to do. No idea what to think. Holden could be lying to her about all of this, but if he wasn't, then he was going to destroy the winery, and there was really no way for her to be sure about which one was true until it was too late.

"Well, what do we do, then?"

"I told you, that is up to you."

"Okay. So say we get married. Then what?"

"You were already prepared to marry a man you didn't love, might as well be me."

Except… This was worse than marrying a man she didn't love.

She had trusted Holden with something deep and real. Some part of her that she had never shown to anyone else. She had trusted him enough to let him tie her hands.

To let him inside her body.

And now she had to make a decision about marrying him. On the heels of discovering that she didn't know him at all.

"I'll marry you," she said. "I'll marry you."

Nine

The roar of victory in Holden's blood hadn't quieted, not even by the time they boarded his private plane. They'd left the party and were now taking off from the regional airport, bound for Las Vegas, and he was amused by the fact that they both just so happened to be dressed for a wedding, though they hadn't planned it.

"Twenty-four-hour wedding chapels and no waiting period," he said, lifting a glass of champagne, and then extending his hand and offering it to her.

The plane was small, but nicely appointed, and fairly quiet.

He wasn't extraordinarily attached to a great many of the creature comforts that had come with his wealth. But being able to go where he wanted, when he wanted, and without a plane full of people was certainly his favorite.

"You have your own plane," she said, taking the glass of champagne and downing it quickly. "You are private-plane rich."

She didn't look impressed so much as pissed.

"Yep," he said.

She shook her head, incredulous. "I… I don't even know what to say to that."

"I didn't ask you to say anything."

"No. You asked me to marry you."

"I believe I *demanded* that you marry me or I'd ruin your family."

"My mistake," she said, her tone acerbic. "How could I be so silly?"

"You may not believe me, but I told you, I didn't intend to involve you in this."

"I just conveniently involved myself?"

"If it helps, I found it an inconvenience at first."

"Why? You felt *guilty*? In the middle of your quest to take down my family and our fortune? Yes, that must've been inconvenient for you."

"I didn't want to drag you into it," he said. "Because I'm not your father. And I sure as hell wasn't going to extract revenge by using you for sex. The sex was separate. I only realized the possibilities when you told me about how your husband would be given an ownership stake in the vineyard."

"Right," she said. "Of course. Because I was an

idiot who thought that since you had been inside me, I could maybe have a casual conversation with you."

"I'm sorry, but the information was too good for me to let go. And in the end, your family gets off easier."

"Except that you might do something drastic and destroy the winery with your control of the share."

"I was absolutely going to do that, but now I can own a piece of it instead. And that benefits me. I also have his daughter, right with me."

"Oh, are you going to hold a gun to my head for dramatics?"

"No gun," he said. "In fact, we're on a private plane, and you're drinking champagne. You're not in any danger from me, and I didn't force you to come with me."

"But you did," she said, her voice thick.

"I offered you two choices."

"I didn't like either of them."

"Welcome to life, princess. You not liking your options isn't the same as you not having any."

She ignored that statement. "This is *not* my life."

"It is now." He appraised her for a long moment, the elegant line of her profile. She was staring out the window, doing her very best not to look at him. "The Big Bad Wolf was always going to try and eat you. You know how the fairy tale goes."

"Say whatever you need to say to make yourself feel better," she said. "You're not a wolf. You're just a dick."

"And your father?"

That seemed to kill her desire to banter with him. "I don't know if I believe you."

"But you believe me just enough to be on a plane with me going to Las Vegas to get married, because if I'm right, if I'm telling the truth…"

"It ruins everything. And I don't think I trust anyone quite so much that I would take that chance. Not even my father. I don't trust you at all, but what choice do I have? Because you're right. I was willing to marry a man that I didn't love to support my family. To support the empire. The dynasty. So why the hell wouldn't I do it now?"

"Oh, but you hate me, don't you?"

"I do," she said. "I really do."

He could sense that there was more she wanted to say, but that she wouldn't. And they were silent for the next hour, until the plane touched down in Nevada.

"Did you want an Elvis impersonator?" he asked, when they arrived on the Strip, at the little white wedding chapel he'd reserved before they landed.

"And me without my phone," she said.

"Did you want to take pictures and post them?"

She narrowed her eyes. "I wanted to beat you over the head with it."

"That doesn't answer my question about Elvis."

"Yeah, that would be good. If we don't have an Elvis impersonator, the entire wedding will be ruined."

"Don't tease me, because I will get the Elvis impersonator."

"Get him," she said, making a broad gesture. "Please. Because otherwise this would be *absurd*."

The edge of hysteria in her voice suggested she felt it was already absurd, but he chose to take what she said as gospel.

And he checked the box on the ridiculous paperwork, requesting Elvis, because she thought he was kidding, and she was going to learn very quickly that he was not a man to be trifled with. Even when it came to things like this.

They waited until their names were called.

And sadly, the only impersonator who was available past ten thirty on a Saturday night seemed to be Elvis from the mid-1970s.

"Do you want me to sing 'Burning Love' or 'Can't Help Falling in Love' at the end of the ceremony?" he asked in all seriousness.

"Pick your favorite," Emerson replied, her face stony.

And Holden knew she had been certain that this level of farce would extinguish the thing that burned between them. Because she hated him now, and he could see the truth of that in her eyes.

But he was happy to accept her challenge. Happy to stand there exchanging vows with an Elvis impersonator as officiant, and a woman in a feathered leotard as witness, because it didn't change the fact that he wanted her.

Desperately.

That all he could think about was when this was finished, he was going to take her up to a lavish suite and have her fifty different ways.

And she might not think she wanted it, but she would.

She might think that she could burn it all out with her anger, but she couldn't. He knew it.

He knew it because he was consumed by it.

He should feel only rage. Should feel only the need for revenge.

But he didn't.

And she wouldn't either.

"You may kiss the bride," Elvis said.

She looked at him with a warning in her eyes, but that warning quickly became a challenge.

She would learn pretty quickly that he didn't back down from a challenge.

He cupped her chin with his hand, and kissed her, hard and fast, but just that light, quick brush of their mouths left them both breathing hard.

And as soon as they separated, the music began to play and Elvis started singing about how he just couldn't help falling in love.

Well, Holden could sure as hell help falling in love. But he couldn't keep himself from wanting Emerson. That was a whole different situation.

They signed the paperwork quickly, and as soon as they were in the car that had been waiting for them, he handed her his phone. "Call your lawyer."

"It's almost midnight," she said.

"He'll take a call from you, you know it. We need to get everything set into motion so we have it all signed tomorrow morning."

"*She* will take a call from me," she said pointedly. But then she did as he asked. "Hi, Julia. It's Emerson. I just got married." He could hear a voice saying indiscriminate words on the other end. "Thank you. I need to make sure that I transfer the shares of the company into my husband's name. As soon as possible." She looked over at him. "Where are we staying?"

She recited all of the necessary information back to Julia at his direction, including the information about him, before getting off the phone.

"She'll have everything faxed to us by morning."

"And she won't tip off your father?"

"No," she said. "She's the family lawyer, but she must know… She's going to realize that I eloped. And she's going to realize that I'm trying to bypass my father. That I want my husband to have the ownership shares he—I—is entitled to. She won't allow my father to interfere."

"She's a friend of yours, then."

"We became friends, yes. People who aren't liars make friends."

"I'm wounded."

"I didn't think you could wound granite."

"Why did you comply with what I asked you to do so easily?"

Suddenly, her voice sounded very small and tired. "Because. It makes no sense to come here, to marry you, if I don't follow through with the rest. You'll ruin my family if you don't get what you asked for. I'm giving it to you. Protesting now is like tying my own self to the railroad tracks, and damsel in distress isn't my style." She looked at him, her blue eyes certain. "I made my bed. I'll lie in it."

They pulled up to the front of a glitzy casino hotel that was far from his taste in anything.

But what he did like about Las Vegas was the sexual excess. Those who created the lavish hotel rooms here understood exactly why a man was willing to pay a lot of money for a hotel room. And it involved elaborate showers, roomy bathtubs and beds that could accommodate all manner of athletics.

The decor didn't matter to him at all with those other things taken into consideration.

They got out of the car, and he tipped the valet.

"Your secretary called ahead, Mr. McCall," the man said. "You're all checked in and ready to go straight upstairs. A code has been texted to your phone."

Holden put his arm around her, and the two of them began to walk to an elevator. "I hope you don't think… I… We're going to a hotel room and…" Emerson said.

"Do you think you're going to share a space with me tonight and keep your hands off me?"

They got inside the elevator, and the doors closed. "I hate you," she said, shoving at his chest.

"And you want me," he said. "And that might make you hate me even more, but it doesn't make it not true."

"I want to…"

"Go ahead," he said. "Whatever you want."

"I'm going to tear that tux right off your body," she said, her voice low and feral. "Absolutely destroy it."

"Only if I can return the favor," he said, arousal coursing through him.

"You might not be all that confident when I have the most fragile part of you in my hand."

He didn't know why, but that turned him on. "I'll take my chances."

"I don't understand what this is," she said. "I should be…disgusted by you."

"It's too late. You already got dirty with me, honey. You might as well just embrace it. Because you know how good it is between us. And you wanted me when I was nothing other than a ranch hand. Why wouldn't you want me when you know that I'm a rich man with a vengeful streak a mile wide?"

"You forced me into this."

"I rescued you from that boring bowl of oatmeal you called a fiancé. At least you hate me. You didn't feel anything for him."

Her hackles were up by the time they got to the

suite door, and he entered his code. The door opened and revealed the lavish room that had all the amenities he wanted out of such a place.

"This is tacky," she said, throwing her purse down on the couch.

"And?"

"Warm," she said.

She reached behind her body and grabbed hold of her zipper, pulling down the tab and letting her dress fall to the floor.

"I figured you were going to make me work for it."

"Your ego doesn't deserve that. Then you'd get to call it a seduction. I want to fuck you, I can't help myself. But I'm not sure you should be particularly flattered by that. I hate myself for it."

"Feel free to indulge your self-loathing, particularly if at some point it involves you getting that pretty lipstick all over me."

"I'm sure it will. Because I'm here with you. And there's not much I can do about my choices now. We're married. And a stake in the vineyard is close to being transferred into your name. I've already had sex with you. I got myself into this. I might as well have an orgasm."

"We can certainly do better than one orgasm," he said.

She looked good enough to eat, standing there in some very bridal underwear, all white and lacy, and unintentionally perfect for the moment, still wearing the red high heels she'd had on with her dress.

He liked her like this.

But he liked her naked even better.

She walked over to where he stood, grabbed hold of his tie and made good on her promise.

She wrenched the knot loose, then tore at his shirt, sending buttons scattering across the floor. "I hope that was expensive," she said, moving her hand over his bare chest.

"It was," he said. "Very, very expensive. But sadly for you, expensive doesn't mean anything to me. I could buy ten more and not notice the expense."

He could see the moment when realization washed over her. About who had the power. She was so very comfortable with her financial status and she'd had an idea about his, and what that meant, and even though she'd seen the plane, seen him in the tux, the reality of who he'd been all along was just now hitting her.

"And to think," she said, "I was very worried about taking advantage of you that night we were together."

"That says more about you and the way you view people without money than it does about me, sweetheart."

"Not because of that. You work for my father. By extension, for me, since I own part of the winery. And I was afraid that I might be taking advantage of you. But here you were, so willing to blackmail me."

"Absolutely. Life's a bastard, and so am I. That's just the way of things."

"Here I thought she was a bitch. Which I've always found handy, I have to say." She pushed his shirt off his shoulders, and he shed it the rest of the way onto the floor, and then she unhooked his belt, pulling it through the loops.

He grinned. "Did you want to use that?"

"What?"

"You know, you could tie me down if you wanted," he said. "If it would make you feel better. Make you feel like you have some control."

Something flared in her eyes, but he couldn't quite read it. "Why would I want that? That wouldn't give me more control. It would just mean I was doing most of the work." She lifted her wrists up in supplication, her eyes never leaving his. "You can tie my wrists, and I'll still have the control."

He put the tip of the leather through the buckle, and looped it over her wrists, pulling the end tight before he looped it through the buckle again, her wrists held fast together. Then, those blue eyes never leaving his, she sank down onto her knees in front of him.

Ten

She had lost her mind, or something. Her heart was pounding so hard, a mixture of arousal, rage and shame pouring over her.

She should have told him no. She should have told him he was never touching her again. But something about her anger only made her want to play these games with him even more, and she didn't know what that said about her.

But he was challenging her, with everything from his marriage proposal to the Elvis at the chapel. This room itself was a challenge, and then the offer to let her tie him up.

All of it was seeing if he could make her or break her, and she refused to break. Because she was Emerson Maxfield, and she excelled at everything she did. And if this was the way she was going to save her family's dynasty, then she was going to save it on her knees in front of Holden McCall.

"You think I'm just going to give you what you want?" he asked, stroking himself through his pants. She could see the aggressive outline of his arousal beneath the dark fabric, and her internal muscles pulsed.

"Yes," she said. "Because I don't think you're strong enough to resist me."

"You might be right about that," he said. "Because I don't do resisting. I spent too much of my life wanting, and that's not something that I allow. I don't want anymore. I have."

He unhooked the closure on his pants, slid the zipper down slowly and then freed himself.

He wrapped his hand around the base, holding himself steady for her. She arched up on her knees and took him into her mouth, keeping her eyes on his the entire time.

With her hands bound as they were, she allowed him to guide her, her hair wrapped around his fist as he dictated her movements.

It was a game.

She could get out of the restraints if she wanted to. Could leave him standing there, hard and aching. But she was submitting to this fiction that she was trapped, because somehow, given the marriage— which she truly was trapped in—this felt like power.

This choice.

Feeling him begin to tremble as she took him in deep, feeling his power fracture as she licked him, tasted him.

She was the one bound, but he couldn't have walked away from her now if he wanted to, and she knew it.

They both did.

He held all the power outside this room, outside this moment. But she'd claimed her own here, and she was going to relish every second.

She teased him. Tormented him.

"Stand up," he said, the words scraping his throat raw.

She looked up at him, keeping her expression serene. "Are you not enjoying yourself?"

"Stand up," he commanded. "I want you to walk to the bed."

She stood slowly, her hands still held in that position of chosen obedience. Then with her eyes never leaving his, she walked slowly toward the bedroom. She didn't turn away from him until she had to, and even then, she could feel his gaze burning into her. Lighting a fire inside of her.

Whatever this was, it was bigger than them both.

Because he hated her father, and whether or not the reasons that he hated James Maxfield were strictly true or not, the fact was he did.

And she didn't get the impression that he was

excited to find himself sexually obsessed with her. But he was.

She actually believed that what he wanted from her in terms of the winery was separate from him wanting her body, because this kind of intensity couldn't be faked.

And most important, it wasn't only on his side.

That had humiliated her at first.

The realization that she had been utterly captivated by this man, even while he was engaged in a charade.

But the fact of the matter was, he was just as enthralled with her.

They were both tangled in it.

Whether they wanted to be or not.

She climbed onto the bed, positioning herself on her back, her arms held straight down in front of her, covering her breasts, covering that space between her thighs. And she held that pose when he walked in.

Hunger lit his gaze and affirmed what she already knew to be true in her heart. He wanted her.

He hated it.

There was something so deliciously wicked about the contrast.

About this control she had over him even now.

A spark flamed inside her stomach.

He doesn't approve of this, or of you. But he can't help himself.

She arched her hips upward unconsciously, seeking some kind of satisfaction.

It was so much more arousing than it had any right to be. This moment of triumph.

Because it was private. Because it was secret.

Emerson lived for appearances.

She had been prepared to marry a man for those appearances.

And yet, this moment with Holden was about nothing more than the desire between two people. That he resented their connection? That only made it all feel stronger, hotter.

He removed his clothes completely as he approached the bed.

She looked down at her own body, realizing she was still wearing her bra and panties, her high heels.

"You like me like this," she whispered.

"I like you any way I can get you," he said, his voice low and filled with gravel.

"You like this, don't you? You had so much commentary on me wanting to slum it with a ranch hand. I think you like something about having a rich girl. Though, now I don't know why."

"Is there any man on earth who doesn't fantasize about corrupting the daughter of his enemy?"

"Did you corrupt me? I must've missed the memo."

"If I haven't yet, honey, then it's going to be a long night." He scooted her up the mattress, and lifted her arms, looping them back over her head, around one of the posts on the bed frame. Her hands parted, the leather from the belt stretching tight over the furniture, holding her fast. "At my mercy," he said.

He took his time with her then.

Took her high heels off her feet slowly, kissing her ankle, her calf, the inside of her thigh. Then he teased the edges of her underwear before pulling them down slowly, kissing her more intimately. He traveled upward, to her breasts, teasing her through the lace before removing the bra and casting it to the floor. And then he stood back, as if admiring his hard work.

"As fun as this is," he said, "I want your hands on me."

She could take her own hands out of the belt, but she refused. Refused to break the fiction that had built between the two of them.

So she waited. Waited as he slowly, painstakingly undid the belt and made a show of releasing her wrists. Her entire body pulsed with need for him. And thankfully, it was Vegas, so there were condoms on the bedside table.

He took care of the necessities, quickly, and then joined her on the bed, pinning her down on the mattress.

She smiled up at him, lifting her hand and tracing the line of his jaw with her fingertip. "Let's go for a ride," she whispered.

He growled, gripped her hips and held her steady as he entered her in one smooth stroke.

She gasped at the welcome invasion, arching against his body as he tortured them both mercilessly, drove them both higher than she thought she could stand.

And when she looked into his eyes, she saw the man she had been with that first night, not a rich stranger.

Holden.

His last name didn't matter. It didn't matter where he was from. What was real was *this*.

And she knew it, because their desire hadn't changed, even if their circumstances had. If anything, their desire had sharpened, grown in intensity.

And she believed with her whole soul that what they'd shared in his bed had never been about manipulating her.

Because the intensity was beyond them. Beyond sex in a normal sense, so much deeper. So much more terrifying.

She took advantage of her freedom. In every sense of the word.

The freedom of her hands to explore every ridge of muscle on his back, down his spine, to his sculpted ass.

And the freedom of being in this moment. A moment that had nothing to do with anything except need.

This…this benefited no one. In fact, it was a short road off a cliff, but that hadn't stopped either of them.

They couldn't stop.

He lowered his head, growling again as he thrust into her one last time, his entire body shaking with his release.

And she followed him over the edge.

She let out a hoarse cry, digging her fingernails into his skin as she crested that wave of desire over and over again.

She didn't think it would end.

She thought she might die.

She thought she might not mind, if this was heaven, between the sheets with him.

And when her orgasm passed, she knew she was going to have to deal with the fact that he was her husband.

With the reality of what her father would think.

With Holden, her father's enemy, owning a share in the winery.

But those realizations made her head pound and her heart ache.

And she would rather focus on the places where her body burned with pleasure.

Tomorrow would come soon enough, and there would be documents to fax and sign, and they would have to fly back to Oregon.

But that was all for later.

And Emerson had no desire to check her phone. No desire to have any contact with the outside world.

No desire to take a picture to document anything.

Because none of this could be contained in a pithy post. None of it could even be summed up in something half so coherent as words.

The only communication they needed was between their bodies.

Tomorrow would require words. Explanations. Probably recriminations.

But tonight, they had this.

And so Emerson shut the world out, and turned to him.

Eleven

By the time he and his new wife were on a plane back to Oregon, Emerson was looking sullen.

"It's possible he'll know what happened by the time we get there," she said.

"But you're confident there's nothing he can do to stop it?"

She looked at him, prickles of irritation radiating off her. A sharp contrast to the willing woman who had been in his bed last night.

"Why do you care? It works out for you either way."

"True. But it doesn't work out particularly well for you."

"And you care about that?"

"I married you."

"Yeah, I still don't really get that. What exactly do you think is going to happen now?"

"We'll have a marriage. Why not?"

"You told me you didn't believe in marriage."

"I also told you I was a ranch hand."

"Have you been married before?" She frowned.

"No. Would it matter if I had?"

"In a practical sense, obviously nothing is a deal breaker, since I'm already married to you, for the winery. So no. But yes. Actually, it does."

"Never been married. No kids."

"Dammit," she said. "It didn't even occur to me that you might have children."

"Well, I don't."

"Thank God."

"Do you want to have some?"

The idea should horrify him. But for some reason, the image of Emerson getting round with his baby didn't horrify him at all. In fact, the side effect of bringing her into his plans pleased him in ways he couldn't quite articulate.

The idea of simply ruining James Maxfield had been risky. Because there was every chance that no matter how hard Holden tried there would be no serious blowback for the man who had harmed Holden's sister the way that he had.

Wealthy men tended to be tougher targets than young women. Particularly young women who traded on the image of their beauty.

Not that Holden wasn't up to the task of trying to ruin the man.

Holden was powerful in his own right, and he was ruthless with it.

But there was something deeply satisfying about owning a piece of his enemy's legacy. And not only that, he got James's precious daughter in the bargain.

This felt right.

"I can't believe that you're suggesting we…"

"You wanted children, right?"

"I… Yes."

"So, it's not such an outrageous thought."

"You think we're going to stay married?"

"You didn't sign a prenuptial agreement, Emerson. You leave me, I still get half of your shares of the vineyard."

"You didn't sign one either. I have the impression half of what's yours comes out to an awful lot of money."

"Money is just money. I'll make more. I don't have anything I care about half as much as you care about the vineyard. About the whole label."

"Well, why don't we wait to discuss children until I decide how much I hate you."

"You hate me so much you climbed on me at least five times last night."

"Yes, and in the cold light of day that seems less exciting than it did last night. The chemistry between us doesn't have anything to do with…our marriage."

"It has everything to do with it," he said, his tone

far darker and more intense than he'd intended it to be.

"What? You manufactured this chemistry so we could…"

"No. The marriage made sense because of our chemistry. I was hardly going to let you walk away from me and marry another man, Emerson. Let him get his hands on your body when he has had all this time? He's had the last two years and he did nothing? He doesn't deserve you. And your father doesn't get to use you as a pawn."

"My father…"

"He's not a good man. Whether you believe me or not, it's true. But I imagine that when we impart the happy news to him today… You can make that decision for yourself."

"Thanks. But I don't need your permission to make my own decisions about my father or anything else."

But the look on her face was something close to haunted, and if he were a man prone to guilt, he might feel it now. They landed not long after, and his truck was there, still where he'd left it.

When they paused in front of it, she gave it a withering stare. "This thing is quite the performance."

It was a pretty beat-up truck. But it was genuinely his.

"It's mine," he said.

"From when?"

"Well, I got it when I was about…eighteen. So going on fifteen years ago."

"I don't even know how old you are. I mean, I do now, because I can do math. But really, I don't know anything about you, Holden."

"Well, I'll be happy to give you the rundown after we meet with your father."

"Well, looking forward to all that."

She was still wearing her dress from last night. He had found a replacement shirt in the hotel shop before they'd left, and it was too tight on his shoulders and not snug enough in the waist. When they arrived at the winery and entered the family's estate together, he could only imagine the picture they made.

Him in part of a tux, and her in last night's gown.

"Is my father in his study yet?" she questioned one of the first members of the household staff who walked by.

"Yes," the woman said, looking between Emerson and him. "Shall I see if he's receiving visitors?"

"He doesn't really have a choice," Holden said. "He'll make time to see us."

He took Emerson's hand and led her through the house, their footsteps loud on the marble floors. And he realized as they approached the office, what a pretentious show this whole place was.

James Maxfield wasn't that different from Holden. A man from humble beginnings hell-bent on forging a different path. But the difference between James and Holden was that Holden hadn't forgotten where he'd come from. He hadn't forgotten what it was to be powerless, and he would never make anyone else feel that kind of desperation.

James seemed to enjoy his position and all the power that came with it.

You don't enjoy it? Is that why you're standing here getting ready to walk through that door with his daughter and make him squirm? Is that why you forced Emerson to marry you?

He pushed those thoughts aside. And walked into the office without knocking, still holding tightly to Emerson.

Her father looked up, looked at him and then at Emerson. "What the hell is this?" he asked.

"I…"

"A hostile takeover," Holden said. "You ruined my sister's life. And now I'm here to make yours very, very difficult. And only by your daughter's good grace am I leaving you with anything other than a smoldering pile of wreckage. Believe me when I say it's not for your sake. But for the innocent people in your family who don't deserve to lose everything just because of your sins."

"Which sins are those?"

"My sister. Soraya Jane."

The silence in the room was palpable. Finally, James spoke.

"What is it you intend to do?"

"You need to guard your office better. I know you think this house isn't a corporation so you don't need high security, but you're such a damned narcissist you didn't realize you'd hired someone who was after the secrets you keep in your home. And now I have them. And thanks to Emerson, I now have a stake in this winery too. You can contest the marriage and my ownership, but it won't end well for you. It might not be my first choice now, but I'm still willing to detonate everything if it suits me."

James Maxfield's expression remained neutral, and his focus turned to his daughter.

"Emerson," her father said, "you agreed to this? You are allowing him to blackmail us?"

"What choice did I have?" she asked, a thread of desperation in her voice. "I trust you, Dad. I do. But he planned to destroy us. Whether his accusations are true or not, that was his intent. He gave me no time, and he didn't give me a lot of options. This marriage was the only way I could salvage what we've built, because he was ready to wage a campaign against you, against our family, at any cost. He was going to come at us personally and professionally. I couldn't take any chances. I couldn't. I did what I had to do. I did what you would have done, I'm sure. I did what needed doing."

"You were supposed to marry Donovan," James said, his tone icy.

"I know," Emerson said. "But what was I supposed to do when the situation changed? This man…"

"Have you slept with him?"

Emerson drew back, clearly shocked that her fa-

ther had asked her that question. "I don't understand
what that has to do with anything."

"It certainly compromises the purity of your
claims," James returned. "You say you've been
blackmailed into this arrangement, but if you're in
a relationship with him…"

"Did you sleep with his sister?" she asked. "All
those… All those other women in the files. Did
you… Did you cheat on Mom?"

"Emerson, there are things you don't need to
know about, and things you don't understand. My
relationship with your mother works, even if it's not
traditional."

"You *did*." She lowered her voice to a near whis-
per. "His sister. She's younger than me."

"Emerson…"

Holden took a step toward James's desk. "Men
like you always think it won't come back on you.
You think you can take advantage of women who
are young, who are desperate, and no one will come
for you. But I am here for you. This empire of yours?
It serves me now. Your daughter? She's mine too.
And if you push me, I swear I will see it all ruined
and everyone will know what you are. How many
people do you think will come here for a wedding,
or parties, then? What of the brand worldwide? Who
wants to think about sexual harassment, coercion
and the destruction of a woman young enough to be
your daughter when they have a sip of your merlot?"

Silence fell, tense and hard between them.

"The brand is everything," James said finally. "I've done everything I can to foster that family brand, as has your mother. What we do in private is between us."

"And the gag order you had my sister sign, and all those other women? Soraya has been institutionalized because of all of this. Because of the fallout. And she might have signed papers, but I did not. And now I don't need to tell the world about your transgressions to have control over what you've built. And believe me, in the years to come, I will make your life hell." Holden leaned forward, placing his palms on the desk. "Emerson was your pawn. You were going to use her as a wife to the man you wanted as part of this empire. But Emerson is with me now. She's no longer yours."

"*Emerson* is right here," Emerson said, her voice vibrating with emotion. "And frankly, I'm disgusted by the both of you. I don't belong to either of you. Dad, I did what I had to do to save the vineyard. I did it because I trusted you. I trusted that Holden's accusations were false. But you did all of this, didn't you?"

"It was an affair," James said. "It looks to me like you are having one of your own, so it's a bit rich for you to stand in judgment of me."

"I hadn't made vows to Donovan. And I never claimed to love him. He also knows…"

"Your mother knows," James said. "The terms of a marriage are not things you discuss with your children. You clearly have the same view of relationships that I do, and here you are lecturing me."

"It's not the same," she said. "And as for you," she said, turning to Holden. "I married you because it was the lesser of two evils. But that doesn't make me yours. You lied to me. You made me believe you were someone you weren't. You're no different from him."

Emerson stormed out of the room, and left Holden standing there with James.

"She makes your victory ring hollow," James said.

"Even if she divorces me, part of the winery is still mine. We didn't have a prenuptial agreement drafted between us, something I'm sure you were intending to take care of when she married that soft boy from the East Coast."

"What exactly are you going to do now?"

"I haven't decided yet. And the beauty of this is I have time. You can consider me the sword of Damocles hanging over your head. And one day, you know the thread will break. The question is when."

"And what do you intend to do to Emerson?"

"I've done it already. She's married to me. She's mine."

Those words burned with conviction, no matter her protests before storming out. And he didn't know why he felt the truth of those words deeper than anything else.

He had married her. It was done as far as he was concerned.

He went out of the office, and saw Emerson standing there, her hands planted firmly on the balustrade, overlooking the entry below.

"Let's talk," he said.

She turned to face him. "I don't want to talk. You should go talk with my father some more. The two of you seemed to be enjoying that dialogue."

"*Enjoy* is a strong word."

"You betrayed me," she said.

"I don't know you, Emerson. You don't know me. We hadn't ever made promises to each other. I didn't betray you. Your *father* betrayed you."

She looked stricken by that, and she said nothing.

"I want you to come live with me."

"Why would I do that?"

"Because we're married. Because it's not fake."

"Does that mean you love me?" she asked, her tone scathing.

"No. But there's a lot of mileage between love and fake. And you know it."

"I live here. I work here. I can't leave."

"Handily, I have bought a property on the adjacent mountain. You won't have to leave. I do have another ranch in Jackson Creek, and I'd like to visit there from time to time. I do a bit of traveling. But there's no reason we can't be based here, in Gold Valley."

"You'll have to forgive me. I'm not understanding the part of your maniacal plan where we try to pretend we're a happy family."

"The vineyard is more yours now than it was before. I have no issue deferring to you on a great many things."

"You're not just going to…let it get run into the ground?"

"If I wanted to do that, I wouldn't have to own a piece. I own part of your father's legacy. And that appeases me.

"So," he concluded, "shall we go?"

Twelve

Emerson looked around the marble halls of the Maxfield estate, and for the very first time in all her life, she didn't feel like she was home.

The man in the office behind her was a stranger.

The man in front of her was her husband, whether or not he was a stranger.

And his words kept echoing in her head.

I didn't betray you. Your father betrayed you.

"Let's go," she said. Before she could think the words through.

She found herself bundled back up into his truck, still wearing the dress she had been wearing at yesterday's party. His house was a quick drive away from the estate, a modern feat of design built into the hillside, all windows to make the most of the view.

"Tell me about your sister," she said, standing in the drive with him, feeling decidedly flat and more than a bit defeated.

"She's my half sister," Holden said, taking long strides toward the front entry. He entered a code, opened the door and ushered her into a fully furnished living area.

"I had everything taken care of already," he said. "It's ready for us."

Ready for us.

She didn't know why she found that comforting. She shouldn't. She was unaccountably wounded by his betrayal, had been forced into this marriage. And yet, she wanted him. She couldn't explain it.

And her old life didn't feel right anymore, because it was even more of a lie than this one.

"My mother never had much luck with love," Holden said, his voice rough. "I had to take care of her. Because the men she was with didn't. They would either abuse her outright or manipulate her, and she wasn't very strong. Soraya came along when I was eight. About the cutest thing I'd ever seen. And a hell of a lot of trouble. I had to get her ready, had to make sure her hair was brushed for school. All of that. But I did it. I worked, and I took care of them, and once I got money, I made sure they had whatever they wanted." He looked away from her, a muscle jumping in his jaw. "It was after Soraya had money that she met your father. I don't think it takes a genius to realize she's got daddy issues. And he played each and every one of them. She got pregnant. He tried to get her to terminate. She wouldn't. She lost the baby anyway. And she lost her mind right along with it."

Hearing those words again, now knowing that they were true…they hit her differently.

She sat down on the couch, her stomach cramping with horror.

"You must love her a lot," she said. "To do all of this for her."

She thought about her father, and how she had been willing to marry a stranger for him. And then how she had married Holden to protect the winery, to protect her family, her father. And now she wasn't entirely convinced she shouldn't have just let Holden do what he wanted.

He frowned. "I did what had to be done. Like I always do. I take care of them."

"Because you love them," she said.

"Because no one else takes care of them." He shook his head. "My family wasn't loving. They still aren't. My mother is one of the most cantankerous people on the face of the planet, but you do what you do. You keep people going. When they're your responsibility, there's no other choice."

"Oh," she said. She took a deep, shuddering breath. "You see, I love my father. I love my mother. That's why her disapproval hurts. That's why his betrayal… I didn't know that he was like this. That he could have done those things to someone like your sister. It hurts me to know it. You're right. He is the one who betrayed me. And I will never be able to go into the estate again and look at it, at him, the same way. I'll never be able to look at him the same. It's just all broken, and I don't think it can ever be put back together."

"We'll see," he said. "I never came here to put anything back together. Because I knew it was all broken beyond the fixing of it. I came here to break *him*, because he broke Soraya. And I don't think she's going to be fixed either." He came to stand in front of Emerson, his hands shoved into his pockets, his expression grim. "And I'm sorry that you're caught up in the middle of this, because I don't have any stake in breaking you. But here's what I know about broken things. They can't be put back together exactly as they were. I think you can make something new out of them, though."

"Are you giving me life advice? Really? The man who blackmailed me into marriage?" He was still so absurdly beautiful, so ridiculously gorgeous and compelling to her. It was wrong. But she didn't know how to fix it. How to change it. Like anything else in her life. And really, right at the moment, it was only one of the deeply messed up things in her reality.

That she felt bonded to him even as the bonds that connected her to her family were shattered.

"You can take it or not," he said. "That doesn't change the fact that it's true. Whether or not I exposed him, your father is a predator. This is who he is. You could have lived your life without knowing the truth, but I don't see how that's comforting."

It wasn't. It made a shiver race down her spine, made her feel cold all over. "I just… I trusted him. I trusted him so much that I was willing to marry a man he chose for me. I would have done anything he asked me to do. He built a life for me, and he gave me a wonderful childhood, and he made me the woman that I am. For better or for worse. He did a whole host of wonderful things for me, and I don't know how to reconcile that with what else I now know about him."

"All *I* know is your father is a fool. Because the way you believe in him… I've never believed in anyone that way. Anyone or anything. And the way my sister believed in him… He didn't deserve that, from either of you. And if just one person believed in me the way that either of you believed in him, the way that I think your mother believes in him, your sisters… I wouldn't have done anything to mess that up."

Something quiet and sad bloomed inside of her. And she realized that the sadness wasn't for losing her faith in her father. Not even a little.

"I did," she said.

"What?"

"I did. Believe in you like that. Holden Brown. That ranch hand I met not so long ago. I don't know what you think about me, or women like me. But it mattered to me that I slept with you. That I let you into my body. I've only been with two other men. For me, sex is an intimate thing. And I've never shared it with someone outside of a relationship. But there was something about you. I trusted you. I believed what you told me about who you were. And I believed in what my body told me about what was between us. And now what we shared has kind of turned into this weird and awful thing, and I just… I don't think I'll ever trust myself again. Between my father and you…"

"I didn't lie to you." His voice was almost furious in its harshness. "Not about wanting you. Nothing that happened between you and me in bed was a lie. Not last night, and not the first night. I swear to you, I did not seduce you to get revenge on your father. Quite the opposite. I told myself when I came here that I would never touch you. You were forbidden to me, Emerson, because I didn't want to do the same thing your father had done. Because I didn't want to lie to you or take advantage of you in any way. When I first met you in that vineyard, I told myself I was disgusted by you. Because you had his blood in your veins. But no matter how much I told myself that, I couldn't make it true. You're not your father. And that's how I feel. This thing between us is separate, and real."

"But the marriage is for revenge."

"Yes. But I wouldn't have taken the wedding *night* if I didn't want you."

"Can I believe in you?"

She didn't know where that question came from,

all vulnerable and sad, and she wasn't entirely sure that she liked the fact that she'd asked it. But she needed to grab on to something. In this world where nothing made sense, in this moment when she felt rootless, because not even her father was who she thought he was, and she didn't know how she was going to face having that conversation with Wren, or with Cricket. Didn't know what she was going to say to her mother, because no matter how difficult their own relationship was, this gave Emerson intense sympathy for her mother.

Not to mention her sympathy for the young woman her father had harmed. And the other women who were like her. How many had there been just like Soraya? It made Emerson hurt to wonder.

She had no solid ground to stand on, and she was desperate to find purchase.

If Holden was telling the truth, if the chemistry between them was as real to him as it was to her, then she could believe in that if nothing else. And she needed to believe in it. Desperately.

"If I… If I go all in on this marriage, Holden, on this thing between us, if we work together to make the vineyard…ours—Wren and Cricket included— promise me that you'll be honest with me. That you will be faithful to me. Because right now, I'll pledge myself to you, because I don't know what the hell else to believe in. I'm angry with you, but if you're telling me the truth about wanting me, and you also told me the truth about my father, then you are the most real and honest thing in my life right now, and I will… I'll bet on that. But only if you promise me right now that you won't lie to me."

"I promise," he said, his eyes like two chips of obsidian, dark and fathomless. Hard.

And in her world that had proven to be built on a shifting sand foundation, his hardness was something steady. Something real.

She needed something real.

She stood up from her position on the couch, her legs wobbling when she closed the distance between them. "Then take me to bed. Because the only thing that feels good right now is you and me."

"I notice you didn't say it's the only thing that makes sense," he said, his voice rough. He cupped her cheek, rubbing his thumb over her cheekbone.

"Because it doesn't make sense. I should hate you. But I can't. Maybe it's just because I don't have the energy right now. Because I'm too sad. But this… whatever we have, it feels *real*. And I'm not sure what else is."

"This *is* real," he said, taking her hand and putting it on his chest. His heart was raging out of control, and she felt a surge of power roll through her.

It was real. Whatever else wasn't, the attraction between them couldn't be denied.

He carried her to the bed, and they said vows to each other's bodies. And somehow, it felt right. Somehow, in the midst of all that she had lost, her desire for Holden felt like the one right thing she had done.

Marrying him. Making this real.

Tonight, there were no restraints, no verbal demands. Just their bodies. Unspoken promises that she was going to hold in her heart forever.

And as the hours passed, a feeling welled up in her chest that terrified her more than anything else.

It wasn't hate. Not even close.

But she refused to give it a name. Not yet. Not now.

She would have a whole lot of time to sort out what she felt for this man.

She'd have the rest of her life.

Thirteen

The day he put Maxfield Vineyards as one of the assets on his corporate holdings was sadistically satisfying. He was going to make a special new label of wine as well. Soraya deserved to be indelibly part of the Maxfield legacy.

Because James Maxfield was indelibly part of Soraya's. And Holden's entire philosophy on the situation was that James didn't deserve to walk away from her without being marked by the experience.

Holden was now a man in possession of a very powerful method through which to dole out if not traditional revenge, then a steady dose of justice.

He was also a man in possession of a wife.

That was very strange indeed. But he counted

his marriage to Emerson among the benefits of this arrangement.

Her words kept coming back to him. Echoing inside of him. All day, and every night when he reached for her.

Can I believe in you?

He found that he wanted her to believe in him, and he couldn't quite figure out why. Why should it matter that he not sweep Emerson into a web of destruction?

Why had he decided to go about marrying her in the first place when he could have simply wiped James Maxfield off the map?

But no. He didn't want to question himself.

Marrying her was a more sophisticated power play. And at the end of the day, he liked it better.

He had possession of the man's daughter. He had a stake in the man's company.

The sword of Damocles.

After all, ruination could be accomplished only once, but this was a method of torture that could continue on for a very long time.

His sense of satisfaction wasn't just because of Emerson.

He wasn't so soft that he would change direction because of a woman he'd slept with a few times.

Though, every night that he had her, he felt more and more connected to her.

He had taken great pleasure a few days ago when she broke the news to her fiancé.

The other man had been upset, but not about Emerson being with another man, rather about the fact that he was losing his stake in the Maxfield dynasty. In Holden's estimation that meant the man didn't deserve Emerson at all. Of course, he didn't care what anyone deserved, not in this scenario. *He* didn't deserve Emerson either, but he wanted her. That was all that mattered to him.

It was more than her ex-fiancé felt for her.

There was one person he had yet to call, though. Soraya. She deserved to know everything that had happened.

He was one of her very few approved contacts. She was allowed to speak to him over the phone.

They had done some very careful and clever things to protect Soraya from contact with the outside world. He, his mother and Soraya's therapists were careful not to cut her off completely, but her social media use was monitored.

They had learned that with people like her, who had built an empire and a web of connections in the digital world, they had to be very careful about cutting them off entirely, or they felt like they had been cast into darkness.

But then, a good amount of their depression often came from that public world.

It was a balance. She was actually on her accounts less now than she had been when she'd first been hospitalized.

He called, and it didn't take long for someone to answer.

"This is Holden McCall. I'm calling for Soraya."

"Your sister is just finishing an art class. She should be with you in a moment."

In art class. He would have never picked something like that for her, but then, her sense of fashion was art in and of itself, he supposed. The way she framed her life and the scenes she found herself in. It was why she was so popular online. That she made her life into art. It pleased him to know she had found another way to express that. One that was maybe about her more than it was about the broader world.

"Holden?" Her voice sounded less frantic, more relaxed than he was used to.

"Yes," he said. "It's me."

"I haven't heard from you in a while." She sounded a bit petulant, childlike and accusing. Which, frankly, was the closest to her old self he'd heard her sound in quite some time.

"I know. I'm sorry. I've been busy. But I have something to tell you. And I hope this won't upset you. I think it might make you happy."

"What is happy?" She said it a bit sharply, and he wondered if she was being funny. It was almost impossible to tell with her anymore.

He ignored that question, and the way it landed inside of him. The way that it hollowed him out.

"I got married," he said.

"Holden," she said, sounding genuinely pleased.

"I'm so glad. Did you fall in love? Love is wonderful. When it isn't terrible."

He swallowed hard. "No. I've married James Maxfield's daughter."

She gasped, the sound sharp in his ear, stabbing him with regret. "Why?"

"Well, that's the interesting part," he said. "I now own some of Maxfield Vineyards. And, Soraya, I'm going to make a wine and name it after you. Because he shouldn't be able to forget you, or what he did to you."

There was silence. For a long moment. "And I'm the one that's locked up because I'm crazy."

"What?"

"Did you hear yourself? You sound… You married somebody you don't love."

"It's not about love. It's about justice. He didn't deserve to get away with what he did to you."

"But he has," she said. "He has because he doesn't care."

"And I've made him care. His daughter knows what kind of man he is now. He's lost a controlling share in his own winery. He's also lost an alliance that he was hoping to build by marrying Emerson off to someone else."

"And the cost of those victories is your happiness. Because you aren't with a woman you love."

"I was never going to fall in love," he said. "It's not in me."

"Yeah, that's what I said too. Money was the only

thing I loved. Until it wasn't." There was another long stretch of silence.

"I thought you would be happy. I'm getting a piece of this for you."

"I don't… I don't want it."

"You don't…"

"You have to do what you have to do," she said.

"I guess so." He didn't know what to say to that, and for the first time since he'd set out on this course, he questioned himself.

"Holden, where is my baby? They won't answer me."

Rage and grief seized up in his chest. She had sounded better, but she wasn't. "Sweetheart," he said. "You lost the baby. Remember?"

The silence was shattering. "I guess I did. I'm sorry. That's silly. It doesn't seem real. I don't seem real sometimes."

And he knew then, that no matter what she said, whether or not she accepted this gift he'd won for her, he didn't regret it. Didn't regret doing this for his sister, who slid in and out of terrible grief so often, and then had to relive her loss over and over again. At least this time she had accepted his response without having a breakdown. But talking about Maxfield cut her every time, he knew.

"Take care of yourself," he said.

"I will," she said.

And he was just thankful that there was someone

there to take care of her, because whatever she said, he worried she wouldn't do it for herself.

And he was resolved then that what he'd done was right.

It had nothing to do with Emerson, or his feelings for her.

James deserved everything that he got and more.

Holden refused to feel guilt about any of it.

Very little had been said between herself and Wren about her elopement. And Emerson knew she needed to talk to her sister. Both of her sisters. But it was difficult to work up the courage to do it.

Because explaining it to them required sharing secrets about their father, secrets she knew would devastate them. She also knew devastating them would further her husband's goals.

Because she and Holden currently had the majority ownership in the vineyard. And with her sisters, they could take absolute control, which she knew was what Holden wanted ultimately.

Frankly, it all made her very anxious.

But anxious or not, talking with her sisters was why she had invited them to have lunch with her down in Gold Valley.

She walked into Bellissima, and the hostess greeted her, recognizing her instantly, and offering her the usual table.

There wasn't much in the way of incredibly fancy dining in Gold Valley, but her family had a good relationship with the restaurants, since they often supplied wine to them, and while they weren't places that required reservations or anything like that, a Maxfield could always count on having the best table in the house.

She sat at her table with a view, morosely perusing the menu while her mouth felt like it was full of sawdust. That was when Cricket and Wren arrived.

"You're actually taking a lunch break," Wren said. "Something must be wrong."

"We need to talk," Emerson said. "I thought it might be best to do it over a basket of bread."

She pushed the basket to the center of the table, like a very tasty peace offering.

Wren eyeballed it. "Things must be terrible if you're suggesting we eat carbs in the middle of the day."

"I eat carbs whenever I want," Cricket said, sitting down first, Wren following her younger sister's lead.

"I haven't really talked to you guys since—"

"Since you defied father and eloped with some guy that none of us even know?" Wren asked.

"Yeah, since that."

"Is he the guy?" Wren asked.

"*What* guy?" Cricket asked.

"She cheated on Donovan, had a one-night stand with some guy that I now assume is the guy she married. And the reason she disappeared from my party the other night."

"You did *what*?" Cricket asked.

"I'm sorry, now you're going to be more shocked about my one-night stand and about my random marriage?"

Cricket blinked. "Well. Yes."

"Yes. It is the same guy."

"Wow," Wren said. "I didn't take you for a romantic, Emerson. But I guess I was wrong."

"No," Emerson said. "I'm not a romantic."

But somehow, the words seemed wrong. Especially with the way her feelings were jumbled up inside of her.

"Then what happened?"

"That's what I need to talk to you about," she said. "It is not a good story. And I didn't want to talk to either of you about it at the winery. But I'm not sure bringing you into a public space to discuss it was the best choice either."

"You do have your own house now," Cricket pointed out.

"Yes. And Holden is there. And... Anyway. It'll all become clear in a second."

Before the waitress could even bring menus to her sisters, Emerson spilled out everything. About their father. About Holden's sister. And about the ultimatum that had led to her marriage.

"You just went along with it?" Wren asked.

"There was no *just* about it," Emerson responded. "I didn't know what he would do to the winery if I didn't comply. And I wasn't sure about Dad's piece in it until...until I talked to him. Holden and I. Dad didn't deny any of it. He says that him and Mom have an understanding, and of course it's something he wouldn't talk about with any of us. But I don't even know if that's true. And my only option is going to Mom and potentially hurting her if I want to find out that truth. So here's what I know so far. That Dad hurt someone. Someone younger than me, someone my new husband loves very much."

"But he's only your husband because he wants to get revenge," Cricket pointed out.

"I… I think that's complicated too. I hope it is."

"You're not in love with him, are you?" Wren asked.

She decided to dodge that question and continue on with the discussion. "I love Dad. And I don't want to believe any of this, but I have to because… it's true."

Cricket looked down. "I wish that I could say I'm surprised. But it's different, being me. I mean, I feel like I see the outside of things. You're both so deep on the inside. Dad loves you, and he pays all kinds of attention to you. I'm kind of forgotten. Along with Mom. And when you're looking at him from a greater distance, I think the cracks show a lot more clearly."

"*I'm* shocked," Wren said sadly. "I've thrown my whole life into this vineyard. Into supporting him. And I… I can't believe that the man who encouraged me, treated me the way he did, could do that to someone else. To many women, it sounds like."

"People and feelings are very complicated," Emerson said slowly. "Nothing has shown me that more than my relationship with Holden."

"You do love him," Wren said.

Did she? Did she love a man who wanted to ruin her family?

"I don't know," Emerson said. "I feel something for him. Because you know what, you're right. I would never have just let him blackmail me into marriage if on some level I didn't… I… It's a real marriage." She felt her face getting hot, which was silly, because she didn't have any hang-ups about that sort of thing normally. "But I'm a little afraid that I'm confusing…well, that part of our relationship being good with actual love."

"I am not the person to consult about that kind of thing," Cricket said, taking a piece of bread out of the basket at the center of the table and biting into it fiercely.

"Don't look at me," Wren said. "We've already had the discussion about my own shameful issues."

Cricket looked at Wren questioningly, but didn't say anything.

"Well, the entire point of this lunch wasn't just to talk about me. Or my feelings. Or Dad. It's to discuss what we are going to do. Because the three of us can band together, and we can make all the controlling decisions for the winery. We supersede my husband even. We can protect the label, keep his actions in check and make our own mark. You're right,

Cricket," Emerson said. "You have been on the out-side looking in for too long. And you deserve better."

"I don't actually want to do anything at the win-ery," Cricket said. "I got a job."

"You did?"

"Yes. At Sugar Cup."

"Making coffee?"

"Yes," Cricket said proudly. "I want to do some-thing different. Different from the whole Maxfield thing. But I'm with you, in terms of banding together for decision-making. I'll be a silent partner, and I'll support you."

"I'm in," Wren said. "Although, you realize that your husband has the ace up his sleeve. He could just decide to ruin us anyway."

"Yes, he could," Emerson said. "But now he owns a piece of the winery, and I think ownership means more to him than that."

"And he has you," Wren pointed out.

"I know," Emerson said. "But what can I do about it?"

"You do love him," Cricket said, her eyes get-ting wide. "I never thought you were sentimental enough."

"To fall in love? I have a heart, Cricket."

"Yes, but you were going to marry when you didn't love your fiancé. It's so patently obvious that you don't have any feelings for Donovan at all, and you were just going to marry him anyway. So, I as-sumed it didn't matter to you. Not really, and now you've gone and fallen in love with this guy… Someone who puts in danger the very thing you care about most. The thing you were willing to marry that bowl of oatmeal for."

"He wasn't a bowl of oatmeal," Emerson said.

"You're right," Wren said. "He wasn't. Because at least a person might want to eat a bowl of oatmeal, even if it's plain. You'd never want to eat him."

"Oh, for God's sake."

"Well," Wren said. "It's true."

"What matters is that the three of us are on the same page. No matter what happens. We are stronger together."

"Right," Wren and Cricket agreed.

"I felt like the rug was pulled out from under me when I found out about Dad. The winery didn't feel like it would ever seem like home again. I felt rootless, drifting. But we are a team. *We* are the Maxfield label. We are the Maxfield name. Just as much as he is."

"Agreed," Wren said.

"Agreed," said Cricket.

And their agreement made Emerson feel some sense of affirmation. Some sense of who she was.

She didn't have the relationship with her father she'd thought she had. She didn't have the father she'd thought she had.

Her relationship with Holden was…

Well, she was still trying to figure it out. But her

relationship with Wren and Cricket was real. And it was strong. Strong enough to weather this, any of it.

And eventually she would have to talk to her mother. And maybe she would find something there that surprised her too. Because if there was one thing she was learning, it was that it didn't matter how things appeared. What mattered was the truth.

Really, as the person who controlled the brand of an entire label using pictures on the internet, she should have known better from the start. But somehow, she had thought that because she was so good at manipulating those images, that she might be immune to falling for them.

Right at this moment she believed in two things: her sisters, and the sexual heat between herself and Holden. Those seemed to be the only things that made any sense. The only things that had any kind of authenticity to them.

And maybe how you feel about him.

Well. Maybe.

But the problem was she couldn't be sure if he felt the same. And just at the moment she was too afraid to take a chance at being hurt. Because she was already raw and wounded, and she didn't know if she could stand anything more.

But she had her sisters. And she would rest in that for now.

Fourteen

The weeks that followed were strange. They were serene in some ways, which Emerson really hadn't expected. Her life had changed, and she was surprised how positive she found the change.

Oh, losing her respect for her father wasn't overly positive. But working more closely with her sisters was. She and Wren had always been close, but both of them had always found it a bit of a challenge to connect with Cricket, but it seemed easier now.

The three of them were a team. It wasn't Wren and Emerson on Team Maxfield, with Cricket hanging out on the sidelines.

It was a feat to launch a new sort of wine on the heels of the select label, which they had only just released. But the only demand Holden had made of the company so far was that they release a line of wines under his sister's name.

Actually, Emerson thought it was brilliant. Soraya had such a presence online—even if she wasn't in the public at the moment—and her image was synonymous with youth. Soraya's reputation gave Emerson several ideas for how to market wines geared toward the youthful jet-set crowd who loved to post photographs of their every move.

One of the first things Emerson had done was consult a graphic designer about making labels that were eminently postable, along with coming up with a few snappy names for the unique blends they would use. And of course, they would need for the price point to be right. They would start with three—Tempranillo Tantrum, Chardonyay and No Way Rosé.

Cricket rolled her eyes at the whole thing, feeling out of step with other people her age, as she had no desire to post on any kind of social media site, and found those puns ridiculous. Wren, while not a big enthusiast herself, at least understood the branding campaign. Emerson was ridiculously pleased. And together the three of them had enjoyed doing the work.

Cricket, true to her word, had not overly involved herself, given that she was in training down at the coffee shop. Emerson couldn't quite understand why her sister wanted to work there, but she could understand why Cricket felt the need to gain some independence.

Being a Maxfield was difficult.

But it was also interesting, building something that wasn't for her father's approval. Sure, Holden's approval was involved on some level, but…this was different from any other work she'd done.

She was doing this as much for herself as for him, and he trusted that she would do a good job. She knew she would.

It felt…good.

The prototype labels, along with the charms she had chosen to drape elegantly over the narrow neck of each bottle, came back from production relatively quickly, and she was so excited to show Holden she could hardly contain herself.

She wasn't sure why she was so excited to show him, only that she was.

It wasn't as if she wanted his approval, the way she had with her father. It was more that she wanted to share what she had created. The way she felt she needed to please him. This was more of an excitement sort of feeling.

She wanted to please Holden in a totally different way. Wanted to make him… Happy.

She wondered what would make a man like him happy. If he *could* be happy.

And suddenly, she was beset by the burning desire to try.

He was a strange man, her husband, filled with dark intensity, but she knew that part of that intensity was an intense capacity to love.

The things that he had done for his sister…

All of her life, really. And for his mother.

It wasn't just this, though it was a large gesture, but everything.

He had protected his mother from her endless array of boyfriends. He had made sure Soraya had gotten off to school okay every day. He had bought his mother and sister houses the moment he had begun making money.

She had done research on him, somewhat covertly, in the past weeks. And she had seen that he had donated large amounts of money, homes, to a great many people in need.

He hid all of that generosity underneath a gruff, hard exterior. Knowing what she knew now, she continually came back to that moment when he had refused to say his plan for revenge was born out of love for his sister. As if admitting to something like love would be disastrous for him.

She saw the top of his cowboy hat through the window of the tasting room, where she was waiting with the Soraya-branded wines.

He walked in, and her heart squeezed tight.

"I have three complete products to show you. And I hope you're going to like them."

She held up the first bottle—the Tempranillo Tantrum—with a little silver porcupine charm dangling from the top. "Because porcupines are grumpy," she said.

"Are they?"

"Well, do you want to hassle one and find out how grumpy they are? Because I don't."

"Very nice," he said, brushing his fingers over the gold foil on the label.

"People will want to take pictures of it. Even if they don't buy it, they're going to post and share it."

He looked at the others, one with a rose-gold unicorn charm, the next with a platinum fox. And above each of the names was *Soraya*.

"She'll love this," he said, his voice suddenly soft.

"How is she doing?"

"Last I spoke to her? I don't know. A little bit better. She didn't seem as confused."

"Do they know why she misremembers sometimes?" He had told her about how his sister often didn't remember she'd had a fairly late-term miscarriage. That sometimes she would call him scared, looking for a baby that she didn't have.

It broke Emerson's heart. Knowing everything Soraya had gone through. And she supposed there were plenty of young women who could have gone through something like that and not ended up in such a difficult position, but Soraya wasn't one of them. And the fact that Emerson's father had chosen someone so vulnerable, and upon learning how vulnerable she was, had ignored the distress she was in…

If Emerson had been on the fence about whether or not her father was redeemable…the more she knew about the state Holden's sister had been left in, the less she thought so.

"Her brain is protecting her from the trauma. Though, it's doing a pretty bad job," he said. "Every time she has to hear the truth again…it hurts her all over."

"Well, I hope this makes her happy," she said, gesturing to the wine. "And that it makes her feel like… she is part of this. Because she's part of the family now. Because of you. My sisters and I… We care about what happens to her. People do care."

"You've done an amazing job with this," he said, the sincerity in his voice shocking her. "I could never have figured out how to make this wine something she specifically would like so much, but this… She's going to love it." He touched one of the little charms. "She'll think those are just perfect."

"I'm glad. I'd like to meet her. Someday. When she is feeling well enough for something like that."

"I'm sure we can arrange it."

After that encounter, she kept turning her feelings over and over inside of her.

She was changing. What she wanted was changing.

She was beginning to like her life with Holden. More than like it. There was no denying the chemistry they shared. That what happened between them at night was singular. Like nothing else she had ever experienced. But it was moments like that one—the little moments that happened during the day—that surprised her.

She liked him.

And if she were really honest with herself, she more than liked him.

She needed…

She needed to somehow show him that she wanted more.

Of course, she didn't know what more there was, considering the fact that they were already married.

She was still thinking about what she wanted, what she could do, when she saw Wren later that day.

"Have you ever been in love?"

Wren looked at her, jerking her head abruptly to the side. "No," she said. "Don't you think you would have known if I'd ever been in love?"

"I don't know. We don't really talk about that kind of stuff. We talk about work. You don't know if I've ever been in love."

"Well, other than Holden? You haven't been. You've had boyfriends, but you haven't been in love."

"I didn't tell you I was in love with Holden."

"But you are," Wren said. "Which is why I assume you're asking me about love now."

"Yes," Emerson said. "Okay. I am. I'm in love with Holden, and I need to figure out a way to tell him. Because how do you tell a man that you want more than marriage?"

"You tell him that you love him."

"It doesn't feel like enough. Anyone can say anything anytime they want. That doesn't make it real. But I want him to see that the way I feel has changed."

"Well, I don't know. Except… Men don't really use words so much as…"

"Sex. Well, our sex life has been good. Very good."

"Glad to hear it," Wren said. "But what might be missing from that?"

Emerson thought about that. "Our wedding night was a bit unconventional." Tearing tuxedos and getting tied up with leather belts might not be everyone's idea of a honeymoon. Though, Emerson didn't really have any complaints.

There had been anger between them that night. Anger that had burned into passion. And since then, they'd had sex in all manner of different ways, because she couldn't be bored when she shared a bed with someone she was so compatible with, and for whatever reason she felt no inhibition when she was with him. But they hadn't had a real wedding night.

Not really.

One where they gave themselves to each other after saying their vows.

That was it. She needed to make a vow to him. With her body, and then with her words.

"I might need to make a trip to town," she said.

"For?"

"Very bridal lingerie."

"I would be happy to knock off work early and help you in your pursuit."

"We really do make a great team."

When she and Wren returned that evening, Emerson was triumphant in her purchases, and more than ready to greet her husband.

Now she just had to hope he would understand what she was saying to him.

And she had to hope he would want the same thing she did.

When Holden got back to the house that night, it was dark.

That was strange, because Emerson usually got home before he did. He was discovering his new work at the winery to be fulfilling, but he also spent a good amount of time dealing with work for his own company, and that made for long days.

He looked down at the floor, and saw a few crimson spots, and for a moment, he knew panic. His throat tightened.

Except... It wasn't blood. It was rose petals.

There was a trail of them, leading from the living room to the stairwell, and up the stairs. He followed the path, down the dimly lit hall, and into the master bedroom that he shared with Emerson.

The rose petals led up to the bed, and there, perched on the mattress, was his wife.

His throat went dry, all the blood in his body rushing south. She was wearing... It was like a bridal gown, but made entirely of see-through lace that gave peeks at her glorious body underneath. The straps were thin, the neckline plunging down between her breasts, which were spilling out over the top of the diaphanous fabric.

She looked like temptation in the most glorious form he'd ever seen.

"What's all this?"

"I… I went to town for a few things today."

"I see that."

"It's kind of a belated wedding gift," she said. "A belated wedding night."

"We had a wedding night. I remember it very clearly."

"Not like this. Not…" She reached next to her, and pulled out a large velvet box. "And we're missing something."

She opened it up, and inside was a thick band of metal next to a slimmer one.

"They're wedding bands," she said. "One for you and one for me."

"What brought this on?"

He didn't really know what to say. He didn't know what to think about this at all.

The past few weeks had been good between the two of them, that couldn't be denied. But he felt like she was proposing to him, and that was an idea he could barely wrap his mind around.

"I want to wear your ring," she said. "And I guess… I bought the rings. But this ring is mine," she said, pulling out the man's ring. "And I want you to wear it. This ring is yours. I want to wear it." She took out the slim band and placed it on her finger, and then held the thicker one out for him.

"I've never been one for jewelry."

"You've never been one for marriage either, but here we are. I know we had a strange start, but this has... It's been a good partnership so far, hasn't it?"

The work she had done on his sister's wine had been incredible, it was true. The care she had put into it had surprised him. It hadn't simply been a generic nod to Soraya. Emerson had made something that somehow managed to capture his sister's whole personality, and he knew Emerson well enough to know that she had done it by researching who Soraya was. And when Emerson asked him about his sister, he knew that she cared. Their own mother didn't even care that much.

But she seemed to bleed with her caring, with her regret that Soraya had been hurt. And now Emerson wanted rings. Wanted to join herself to him in a serious way.

And why not? She's your wife. She should be wearing your ring.

"Thanks," he said, taking the ring and putting it on quickly.

Her shoulders sagged a little, and he wondered if she had wanted this to go differently, but he was wearing the ring, so it must be okay. She let out a shaking breath. "Holden, with this ring, I take you as my husband. To have and to hold. For better or for worse. For richer or poorer. Until death separates us."

Those vows sent a shiver down his spine.

"We took those vows already."

"I took those vows with you because I had to. Because I felt like I didn't have another choice. I'm saying them now because I choose to. Because I want to. And because I mean them. If all of this, the winery, everything, goes away, I still want to be partners with you. In our lives. Not just in business. I want this to be about more than my father, more than your sister. I want it to be about us. And so that's my promise to you with my words. And I want to make that official with my body."

There were little ties at the center of the dress she was wearing, and she began to undo the first one, the fabric parting between her breasts. Then she undid the next one, and the next, until it opened, revealing the tiny pair of panties she had on underneath. She slipped the dress from her shoulders and then she began to undress him.

It was slow, unhurried. She'd torn the clothes from his body before. She had allowed him to tie her hands. She had surrendered herself to him in challenging and intense ways that had twisted the idea of submission on its head, because when her hands were tied, he was the one that was powerless.

But this was different. And he felt…

Owned.

By that soft, sweet touch, by the brush of her fingertips against him as she pushed his shirt up over his head. By the way her nimble fingers attacked his belt buckle, removing his jeans.

And somehow, *he* was the naked one then, and she was still wearing those panties. There was something generous about what she was doing now. And he didn't know why that word came to the front of his mind.

But she was giving.

Giving from a deep place inside of her that was more than just a physical gift. Without asking for anything in return. She lay back on the bed, lifting her hips slightly and pushing her panties down, revealing that tempting triangle at the apex of her thighs, revealing her whole body to him.

He growled, covering her, covering her mouth with his own, kissing her deep and hard.

And she opened to him. Pliant and willing.

Giving.

Had anyone ever given to him before?

He'd had nothing like this ever. That was the truth.

Everyone in his life had taken from him from the very beginning. But not her. And she had no reason to give to him. And if this were the same as all their other sexual encounters, he could have put it off to chemistry.

Because everybody was a little bit wild when there was sexual attraction involved, but this was more.

Sex didn't require vows.

It didn't require rings.

And it didn't feel like this.

This was more.

It touched him deeper, in so many places deep inside, all the way to his soul.

And he didn't know what to say, or feel, so he just kissed her. Because he knew how to do that. Knew how to touch her and make her wet. Knew how to make her come.

He knew how to find his pleasure in her.

But he didn't know how to find the bottom of this deep, aching need that existed inside of him.

He settled himself between her thighs, thrust into her, and she cried out against his mouth. Then her gaze met his, and she touched him, her fingertips skimming over his cheekbone.

"I love you." The words were like an arrow straight through his chest.

"Emerson…"

She clung to him, grasping his face, her legs wrapped around his. "I love you," she said, rocking up into him, taking him deeper.

And he would have pulled away, done something to escape the clawing panic, but his desire for her was too intense.

Love.

Had anyone ever said those words to him? He didn't think so. He should let go of her, he should stop. But he was powerless against the driving need to stay joined to her. It wasn't even about release. It was about something else, something he couldn't name or define.

Can't you?

He ignored that voice. He ignored that burning sensation in his chest, and he tried to block out the words she'd said. But she said them over and over again, and something in him was so hungry for them, he didn't know how to deny himself.

He looked down, and his eyes met hers, and he was sure she could see straight inside of him, and that what she saw there would be woefully empty compared to what he saw in hers.

He growled, lowering his head and chasing the pleasure building inside of him, thrusting harder, faster, trying to build up a pace that would make him forget.

Who he was.

What she'd said.

What he wanted.

What he couldn't have.

But when her pleasure crested, his own followed close behind, and he made the mistake of looking at her again. Of watching as pleasure overtook her.

He had wanted her from the beginning.

It had never mattered what he could get by marrying her.

It had always been about her. Always.

Because he had seen her, and he could not have her, from the very first.

He had told himself he should hate her because

she had Maxfield blood in her veins. Then he had told himself that he needed her, and that was why it had to be marriage.

But he was selfish, down to his core.

And he had manipulated, used and blackmailed her. He was no different than her father, and now here she was, professing her love. And he was a man who didn't even know what that was.

All this giving. All this generosity from her. And he didn't deserve it. Couldn't begin to.

And he deserved it from her least of all.

Because he had nothing to give back.

He shuddered, his release taking him, stealing his thoughts, making it impossible for him to feel anything but pleasure. No regrets. No guilt. Just the bliss of being joined to her. And when it was over, she looked at him, and she whispered one more time, "I love you."

And that was when he pulled away.

Fifteen

She had known it was a mistake, but she hadn't been able to hold it back. The declaration of love. Because she did love him. It was true. With all of herself. And while she had been determined to show him, with her body, with the vows she had made and with the rings she had bought, it wasn't enough.

She had thought the words by themselves wouldn't be enough, but the actions without the words didn't mean anything either. Not to her. Not when there was this big shift inside her, as real and deep as anything ever had been. She had wanted for so long to do enough that she would be worthy. And she felt like some things had crystallized inside of her. Because all of those things she craved, that approval, it was surface. It was like a brand. The way that her father saw brand. That as long as the outside looked good, as long as all the external things were getting done, that was all that mattered.

But it wasn't.

Because what she felt, who she was in her deepest parts, those were the things that mattered. And she didn't have to perform or be good to be loved. She, as a person, was enough all on her own. And that was what Holden had become to her. And that was what she wanted. For her life, for her marriage. Not something as shallow as approval for a performance. A brand was meaningless if there was no substance behind it. A beautiful bottle of wine didn't matter if what was inside was nothing more than grape juice.

A marriage was useless if love and commitment weren't at the center.

It was those deep things, those deep connections, and she hadn't had them, not in all her life. Not really. She was beginning to forge them with her sisters, and she needed them from Holden.

And if that meant risking disapproval, risking everything, then she would. She had. And she could see that her declaration definitely hadn't been the most welcome.

Since she'd told him she loved him, everything about him was shut down, shut off. She knew him well enough to recognize that.

"I don't know what you expect me to say."

"Traditionally, people like to hear 'I love you too.' But I'm suspecting I'm not going to get that. So, here's the deal. You don't have to say anything. I just… I wanted you to know how I felt. How serious I am. How much my feelings have changed since I first met you."

"Why?"

"Because," she said. "Because you…you came into my life and you turned it upside down. You uncovered so many things that were hidden in the dark for so long. And yes, some of that uncovering has been painful. But more than that, you made me realize what I really wanted from life. I thought that as long as everything looked okay, it would be okay. But you destroyed that. You destroyed the illusions all around me, including the ones I had built for myself. Meeting you, feeling that attraction for you, it cut through all this…bullshit. I thought I could marry a man I didn't even feel a temptation to sleep with. And then I met you. I felt more for you in those few minutes in the vineyard that night we met than I had felt for Donovan in the two years we'd been together. I couldn't imagine not being with you. It was like an obsession, and then we were together, and you made me want things, made me do things that I never would have thought I would do. But *those* were all the real parts of me. All that I am.

"I thought that if I put enough makeup on, and smiled wide enough, and put enough filters on the pictures, that I could be the person I needed to be, but it's not who I am. Who I am is the woman I am when I'm with you. In your arms. In your bed. The things you make me feel, the things you make me want. That's real. And it's amazing, because none of this is about optics, it's not about pleasing anyone, it's just about me and you. It's so wonderful. To have found this. To have found you."

"You didn't find me, honey. I found you. I came here to get revenge on your father. This isn't fate. It was calculated through and through."

"It started that way," she said. "I know it did. And I would never call it fate. Because I don't believe that it was divine design that your sister was injured the way that she was. But what I do believe is that there has to be a way to make something good out of something broken, because if there isn't, then I don't know what future you and I could possibly have."

"There are things that make sense in this world," he said. "Emotion isn't one of them. Money is. What we can do with the vineyard, that makes sense. We can build that together. We don't need any of the other stuff."

"The other stuff," she said, "is only everything. It's only love. It took me until right now to realize that. It's the missing piece. It's what I've been looking for all this time. It really is. And I… I love you. I love you down to my bones. It's real. It's not about a hashtag or a brand. It's about what I feel. And how it goes beyond rational and reasonable. How it goes beyond what should be possible. I love you. I love you and it's changed the way that I see myself."

"Are you sure you're not just looking for approval

from somewhere else? You lost the relationship with your father, and now…"

"You're not my father. And I'm not confused. Don't try to tell me that I am."

"I don't do love," he said, his voice hard as stone.

"Somehow I knew you would say that. You're so desperate to make me believe that, aren't you? Mostly because I think you're so desperate to make yourself believe it. You won't even admit that you did all of this because you love your sister."

"Because you are thinking about happy families, and you're thinking about people who share their lives. That's never been what I've had with my mother and sister. I take care of them. And when I say that, I'm telling you the truth. It's not… It's not give-and-take."

"You loving them," she said, "and them being selfish with that love has nothing to do with who you are. Or what you're capable of. Why can't we have something other than that? Something other than me trying to earn approval and you trying to rescue? Can't we love each other? Give to each other? That's what I want. I think our bodies knew what was right all along. I know why you were here, and what you weren't supposed to want. And I know what I was supposed to do. But I think we were always supposed to be with each other. I do. From the deepest part of my body. I believe that."

"Bodies don't know anything," he said. "They

just know they want sex. That's not love. And it's not anything worth tearing yourself apart over."

"But I... I don't have another choice. I'm torn apart by this. By us. By what we could be."

"There isn't an us. There is you and me. And we're married, and I'm willing to make that work. But you have to be realistic about what that means to a man like me."

"No," Emerson said. "I refuse to be realistic. Nothing in my life has ever been better because I was realistic. The things that have been good happened because I stepped out of my comfort zone. I don't want to be trapped in a one-sided relationship. To always be trying to earn my place. I've done that. I've lived it. I don't want to do it anymore."

"Fair enough," he said. "Then we don't have to do this."

"No," she said. "I want our marriage. I want..."

"You want me to love you, and I can't. I'm sorry. But I can't, I won't. And I..." He reached out, his callused fingertips skimming her cheek. "Honey, I appreciate you saying I'm not like your father, but it's pretty clear that I am. I'm not going to make you sign a nondisclosure agreement or anything like that. I'm going to ask one thing of you. Keep the Soraya wine going for my sister. But otherwise, my share of the winery goes to you."

"What?"

"I'm giving it back. I'm giving it to you. Because it's yours, it's not mine."

"You would rather…do all of that than try to love me?"

"I never meant to hurt you," he said. "That was never my goal, whether you believe it or not. I don't have strong enough feelings about you to want to hurt you."

And those words were like an arrow through her heart, piercing deeper than any other cruelty that could have come out of his mouth.

It would've been better, in fact, if he had said that he hated her. If he had threatened to destroy the winery again. If her ultimatum had made him fly into a rage. But it didn't. Instead, he was cold, closed off and utterly impassive. Instead, he looked like a man who truly didn't care, and she would've taken hatred over that any day, because it would have meant that at least he felt something. But she didn't get that. Instead, she got a blank wall of nothing.

She couldn't fight this. Couldn't push back against nothing. If he didn't want to fight, then there was nothing for her to do.

"So that's it," she said. "You came in here like a thunderstorm, ready to destroy everything in your path, and now you're just…letting me go?"

"Your father is handled. The control of the winery is with you and your sisters. I don't have any reason to destroy you."

"I don't think that you're being chivalrous. I think you're being a coward."

"Cowards don't change their lives, don't make

something of themselves the way I did. Cowards don't go out seeking justice for their sisters."

"Cowards *do* run when someone demands something that scares them, though. And that's what you're doing. Make no mistake. You can pretend you're a man without fear. You're hard in some ways, and I know it. But all that hardness is just to protect yourself. I wish I knew why. I wish I knew what I could do."

"It won't last," he said. "Whatever you think you want to give me, it won't last."

"Why do you think that?"

"I've never actually seen anyone want to do something that wasn't ultimately about serving themselves. Why would you be any different?"

"It's not me that's different. It's the feelings."

"But you have to be able to put your trust in feelings in order to believe in something like that, and I don't. I believe in the things you can see, in the things you can buy."

"I believe in us," she said, pressing her hand against her chest.

"You believe wrong, darlin'."

Pain welled up inside of her. "You're not the Big Bad Wolf after all," she said. "At least he had the courage to eat Red Riding Hood all up. You don't even have the courage to do that."

"You should be grateful."

"You don't get to break my heart and tell me I should be grateful because you didn't do it a certain way. The end result is the same. And I hope that someday you realize you broke your own heart too. I hope that someday you look back on this and realize we had love, and you were afraid to take it. And I hope you ask yourself why it was so much easier for you to cross a state because of rage than it was for you to cross a room and tell someone you love them."

She started to collect her clothes, doing her very best to move with dignity, to keep her shoulders from shaking, to keep herself from dissolving. And she waited. As she collected her clothes. Waited for her big, gruff cowboy to sweep her up in his arms and stop her from leaving. But he didn't. He let her gather her clothes. And he let her walk out the bedroom door. Let her walk out of the house. Let her walk out of his life. And as Emerson stood out in front of the place she had called home with a man she had come to love, she found herself yet again unsure of what her life was.

Except… Unlike when the revelations about her father had upended everything, this time she had a clear idea of who *she* was.

Holden had changed her. Had made her realize the depth of her capacity for pleasure. For desire. For love. Had given her an appreciation of depth.

An understanding of what she could feel if she dug deep, instead of clinging to the perfection of the surface.

And whatever happened, she would walk away

from this experience changed. Would walk away from this wanting more, wanting better.

He wouldn't, though.

And of all the things that broke her heart in this moment, that truth was the one that cut deepest.

Emerson knew she couldn't avoid having a conversation with her mother any longer. There were several reasons for that. The first being that she'd had to move back home. The second being that she had an offer to make her father. But she needed to talk to her mom about it first.

Emerson took a deep breath, and walked into the sitting room, where she knew she would find her mother at this time of day.

She always took tea in the sitting room with a book in the afternoon.

"Hi," she said. "Can we talk?"

"Of course," her mom said, straightening and setting her book down. "I didn't expect to see you here today."

"Well. I'm kind of…back here. Because I hit a rough patch in my marriage. You know, by which I mean my husband doesn't want to be married to me anymore."

"That is a surprise."

"Is it? I married him quickly, and really not for the best reasons."

"It seemed like you cared for him quite a bit."

"I did. But the feeling wasn't mutual. So there's not much I can do about that in any case."

"We all make choices. Although, I thought you had finally found your spine with this one."

Emerson frowned. "My spine?"

"Emerson, you have to understand, the reason I've always resisted your involvement in the winery is because I didn't want your father to own you."

"What are you talking about?"

"I know you know. The way that he is. It's not a surprise to me, I've known it for years. He's never been faithful to me. But that's beside the point. The real issue is the way that he uses people."

"You've known. All along?"

"Yes. And when I had you girls the biggest issue was that if I left, he would make sure that I never saw you again. That wasn't a risk I could take. And I won't lie to you, I feared poverty more than I should have. I didn't want to go back to it. And so I made some decisions that I regret now. Especially as I watched you grow up. And I watched the way he was able to find closeness with you and with Wren. When I wasn't able to."

"I just… No matter what I did, you never seemed like you thought I did enough. Or like I had done it right."

"And I'm sorry about that. I made mistakes. In pushing you, I pushed you away, and I think I pushed you toward your father. Which I didn't mean to do. I was afraid, always, and I wanted you to be able to stand on your own feet because I had ended up hobbling myself. I was dependent on his money. I didn't know how to do anything separate from this place, separate from him that could keep me from sinking back into the poverty that I was raised in. I was trapped in many ways by my own greed. I gave up so much for this. For him." Her eyes clouded over. "That's another part of the problem. When I chose your father over… When I chose your father, it was such a deep, controversial thing, it caused so much pain, to myself included, in many ways, and I'm too stubborn and stiff-necked to take back that kind of thing."

"I don't understand."

She ran a hand over her lined brow, pushing her dark hair off her face. "I was in love with someone else. There was a misunderstanding between us, and we broke up. Then your father began to show an interest, because of a rivalry he had with my former beau. I figured that I would use that. And it all went too far. This is the life I made for myself. And what I really wanted, to try and atone for my sins, was to make sure you girls had it different. But then he was pushing you to marry… So when you came back from Las Vegas married to Holden, what I hoped was that you had found something more."

Emerson was silent for a long moment, trying to process all this information. And suddenly, she saw everything so clearly through her mother's eyes. Her fears, the reason she had pushed Emerson the way she had. The way she had disapproved of Emerson pouring everything into the winery.

"I do love Holden," Emerson said. "But he...he says he doesn't love me."

"That's what happened with the man I loved. And I got angry, and I went off on my own. Then I went to someone else. I've always regretted it. Because I've never loved your father the way that I loved him. Then it was too late. I held on to pride, I didn't want to lower myself to beg him to be with me, but now I wish I had. I wish I had exhausted everything in the name of love. Rather than giving so much to stubbornness and spite. To financial security. Without love, these sorts of places just feel like a mausoleum. A crypt for dead dreams." She smiled sadly, looking around the vast, beautiful room that seemed suddenly so much darker. "I have you girls. And I've never regretted that. I have regretted our lack of closeness, Emerson, and I know that it's my fault."

"It's mine too," Emerson said. "We've never really talked before, not like this."

"There wasn't much I could tell you. Not with the way you felt about your father. And... You have to understand, while I wanted to protect you, I also didn't want to shatter your love for him. Because no matter what else he has done, he does love his daughters. He's a flawed man, make no mistake. But what he feels for you is real."

"I don't know that I'm in a place where that can matter much to me."

"No, I don't suppose you are. And I don't blame you."

"I want to buy Dad out of the winery," Emerson said. "When Holden left, he returned his stake to me. I want to buy Dad out. I want to run the winery with Wren and Cricket. And there will be a place here for you, Mom. But not for him."

"He's never going to agree to that."

"If he doesn't, I'll expose him myself. Because I won't sit by and allow the abuse of women and of his power to continue. He has two choices. He can leave of his own accord, or I'll burn this place to the ground around me, but I won't let injustice go on."

"I didn't have to worry about you after all," her mother said. "You have more of a spine than I've ever had."

"Well, now I do. For this. But when it comes to Holden…"

"Your pride won't keep you warm at night. And you can't trade one man for another, believe me, I've tried. If you don't put it all on the line, you'll regret it. You'll have to sit by while he marries someone else, has children with her. And everything will fester inside of you until it turns into something dark and ugly. Don't let that be you. Don't make the mistakes that I did."

"Mom… Who…"

"It doesn't matter now. It's been so long. He probably doesn't remember me anyway."

"I doubt that."

"All right, he remembers me," she said. "But not fondly."

"I love him," Emerson said. "I love him, and I don't know what I'm going to do without him. Which is silly, because I've lived twenty-nine years without him. You would think that I would be just fine."

"When you fall in love like that, you give away a piece of yourself," her mom said. "And that person always has it. It doesn't matter how long you had them for. When it's real, that's how it is."

"Well, I don't know what I'm supposed to do."

"Hope that he gave you a piece of him. Hope that whatever he says, he loves you just the way you love him. And then do more than hope. You're strong enough to come in here and stand up to your father. To do what's right for other people. Do what's right for you too."

Emerson nodded slowly. "Okay." She looked around, and suddenly laughter bubbled up inside of her.

"What?"

"It's just… A few weeks ago, at the launch for the select label, I was thinking how bored I was. Looking forward to my boring future. My boring marriage. I would almost pay to be bored again, because at least I wasn't heartbroken."

"Oh, trust me," her mom said. "As painful as it is, love is what gets you through the years. Even if you don't have it anymore. You once did. Your heart remembers that it exists in the world, and then suddenly the world looks a whole lot more hopeful. Because when you can believe that two people from completely different places can come together and find something that goes beyond explanation, something that goes beyond what you can see with your eyes…that's the thing that gives you hope in your darkest hour. Whatever happens with him…"

"Yeah," Emerson said softly. "I know."

She did. Because he was the reason she was standing here connecting with her mother now. He was the reason she was deciding to take this action against her father.

And she wouldn't be the reason they didn't end up together. She wouldn't give up too soon.

She didn't care how it looked. She would go down swinging.

Optics be damned.

Sixteen

Holden wasn't a man given to questioning himself. He acted with decisiveness, and he did what had to be done. But his last conversation with Emerson kept replaying itself in his head over and over again. And worse, it echoed in his chest, made a terrible, painful tearing sensation around his heart every time he tried to breathe. It felt like... He didn't the hell know. Because he had never felt anything like it before. He felt like he had cut off an essential part of himself and left it behind and it had nothing to do with revenge.

He was at the facility where his sister lived, visiting her today, because it seemed like an important thing to do. He owed her an apology.

He walked through the manicured grounds and up to the front desk. "I'm here to see Soraya Jane."

The facility was more like high-end apartments, and his sister had her rooms on the second floor, overlooking the ocean. When he walked in, she was sitting there on the end of the bed, her hair loose.

"Good to see you," he said.

"Holden."

She smiled, but she didn't hug him.

They weren't like that.

"I came to see you because I owe you an apology."

"An apology? That doesn't sound like you."

"I know. It doesn't."

"What happened?"

"I did some thinking and I realized that what I did might have hurt you more than it helped you. And I'm sorry."

"You've never hurt me," she said. "Everything you do is just trying to take care of me. And nobody else does that."

He looked at his sister, so brittle and raw, and he realized that her issues went back further than James Maxfield. She was wounded in a thousand ways, by a life that had been more hard knocks than not. And she was right. No one had taken care of her but him. And he had been the oldest, so no one had taken care of him at all.

And the one time that Soraya had tried to reach out, the one time she had tried to love, she had been punished for it.

No wonder it had broken her the way it had.

"I abandoned my revenge plot. Emerson and I are going to divorce."

"You don't look happy," she said.

"I'm not," he said. "I hurt someone I didn't mean to hurt."

"Are you talking about me or her?"

He was quiet for a moment. "I didn't mean to hurt either of you."

"Did you really just marry her to get back at her father?"

"No. Not only that. I mean, that's not why I married her."

"You look miserable."

"I am, but I'm not sure what that has to do with anything."

"It has to do with love. This is how love is. It's miserable. It makes you crazy. And I can say that."

"You're not crazy," he said, fiercely. "Don't say that about yourself, don't think it."

"Look where I am."

"It's not a failure. And it doesn't… Soraya, there's no shame in having a problem. There's no shame in getting help."

"Fine. Well, what's your excuse then? I got help and you ruined your life."

"I'm not in love."

"You're not? Because you have that horrible look about you. You know, like someone who just had their heart utterly ripped out of their chest."

He was quiet for a moment, and he took a breath.

He listened to his heart beat steadily in his ears. "My heart is still there," he said.

"Sure. But not your *heart* heart. The one that feels things. Do you love her?"

"I don't know how to love people. How would we know what real, healthy love looks like? I believe that you loved James Maxfield, but look where it got you. Weird… We are busted up and broken from the past, how are we supposed to figure out what's real?"

"If it feels real, it is real. I don't think there's anything all that difficult to understand about love. When you feel like everything good about you lives inside another person, and they're wandering around with the best of you in their chest, you just want to be with them all the time. And you're so afraid of losing them, because if you do, you're going to lose everything interesting and bright about you too."

He thought of Emerson, of the way she looked at him. And he didn't know if what Soraya said was true. If he felt like the best of him was anywhere at all. But what he knew for sure was that Emerson made him want to be better. She made him want something other than money or success. Something deep and indefinable that he couldn't quite grasp.

"She said she loved me," he said, his voice scraped raw, the admission unexpected.

"And you left her?"

"I forced her to marry me. I couldn't…"

"She loves you. She's obviously not being forced into anything."

"I took advantage…"

"You know, if you're going to go worrying about taking advantage of women, it might be helpful if you believe them when they tell you what they want. You deciding that you know better than she does what's in her heart is not enlightened. It's just more of some man telling a woman what she ought to be. And what's acceptable for her to like and want."

"I…" He hadn't quite expected that from his sister.

"She loves you. If she loves you, why won't you be with her?"

"I…"

He thought about what Emerson had said. When she called him a coward.

"Because I'm afraid I don't know how to be in love," he said finally.

It was the one true thing he'd said on the matter. He hadn't meant to lie, he hadn't known that he had. But it was clear as day to him now.

"Look at how we were raised. I don't know a damn thing about love."

"You're the only one who ever did," Soraya said. "Look what you've done for me. Look at where I am. It's not because of me."

"No," he said. "It's because of me. I got you started on all the modeling stuff, and you went to the party where you met James…"

"That's not what I meant. I meant the reason that I'm taken care of now, the reason that I've always been taken care of, is because of you. The reason

Mom has been taken care of… That's you. All those families you gave money to, houses to. And I know I've been selfish. Being here, I've had a lot of time to think. And I know that sometimes I'm not…lucid. But sometimes I am, and when I am, I think a lot about how much you gave. And no one gave it back to you. And I don't think it's that you don't know how to love, Holden. I think it's that you don't know what it's like when someone loves you back. And you don't know what to do with it."

He just sat and stared, because he had never thought of himself the way that his sister seemed to. But she made him sound…well, kind of like not a bad guy. Maybe even like someone who cared quite a bit.

"I don't blame you for protecting yourself. But this isn't protecting yourself. It's hurting yourself."

"You might be right," he said, his voice rough. "You know, you might be right."

"Do you love her?"

He thought about the way Emerson had looked in the moments before he had rejected her. Beautiful and bare. His wife in every way.

"Yes," he said, his voice rough. "I do."

"Then none of it matters. Not who her father is, not being afraid. Just that you love her."

"Look what it did to you to be in love," he said. "Don't you think I'm right to be afraid of it?"

"Oh," she said. "You're definitely right to be afraid of it. It's terrifying. And it has the power to destroy everything in its path. But the alternative is this. This kind of gray existence. The one that I'm in. The one that you're in. So maybe it won't work out. But what if it did?"

And suddenly, he was filled with a sense of determination. With a sense of absolute certainty. There was no what-if. Because he could make it turn out with his actions. He was a man who had—as Emerson had pointed out—crossed the state for revenge.

He could sure as hell do the work required to make love last. It was a risk. A damn sight bigger risk than being angry.

But he was willing to take it.

"Thank you," he said to his sister.

"Thank you too," she said. "For everything. Even the revenge."

"Emerson is making a wine label for you," he said. "It's pretty brilliant."

Soraya smiled. "She is?"

"Yes."

"Well, I can't wait until I can come and celebrate with the both of you."

"Neither can I."

And now all that was left was for him to go and make sure he had Emerson, so the two of them could be together for the launch of the wine label, and for the rest of forever.

Emerson was standing on the balcony to her bedroom, looking out over the vineyard.

It was hers now, she supposed. Hers and Wren's

and Cricket's. The deal with her father had been struck, and her mother had made the decision to stay there at the winery, and let James go off into retirement. The move would cause waves; there was no avoiding it. Her parents' separation, and her father removing himself from the label.

But Emerson had been the public face of Maxfield for so long that it would be a smooth enough transition.

The moonlight was casting a glow across the great fields, and Emerson sighed, taking in the simple beauty of it.

Everything still hurt, the loss of Holden still hurt. But she could already see that her mother was right. Love was miraculous, and believing in the miraculous, having experienced it, enhanced the beauty in the world, even as it hurt.

And then, out in the rows, she was sure that she saw movement.

She held her breath, and there in the moonlight she saw the silhouette of a cowboy.

Not just a cowboy. *Her* cowboy.

For a moment, she thought about not going down. She thought about staying up in her room. But she couldn't. She had to go to him.

Even if it was foolish.

She stole out and padded down the stairs, out the front door of the estate and straight out to the vines.

"What are you doing here?"

"I know I'm not on the guest list," he said.

"No," she said. "You're not. In fact, you were supposed to have ridden off into the sunset."

"Sorry about that. But the sun has set."

"Holden…"

"I was wondering if you needed a ranch hand."

"What?"

"The winery is yours. I want it to stay yours. Yours and your sisters'. I certainly don't deserve a piece of it. And I just thought… The one time I had it right with you was when I worked here. When it was you and me, and not all this manipulation. So I thought maybe I would just offer me."

"Just you?"

"Yeah," he said. "Just me."

"I mean, you still have your property development money, I assume."

"Yeah," he said. "But… I also love you. And I was sort of hoping that you still love me."

She blinked hard, her heart about to race out of her chest. "Yes," she said. "I love you still. I do. And all I need is you. Not anything else."

"I feel the same way," he said. "You. Just the way you are. It quit being about revenge, and when it quit being about revenge, I didn't have an excuse to stay anymore, and it scared the hell out of me. Because I never thought that I would be the kind of man that wanted forever. And wanting it scared me. And I don't like being scared."

"None of us do. But I'm so glad that you came here, though," she said. "Because if you hadn't… I thought as long as everything looked good, then it was close enough to being good. I had no idea that it could be like this."

"And if I had never met you, then I would never have had anything but money and anger. And believe me, compared to this, compared to you, that's nothing."

"You showed me my heart," she said. "You showed me what I really wanted."

"And you showed me mine. I was wrong," he said. "When I said things couldn't be fixed. They can be. When I told my sister that I came here to get revenge, she wasn't happy. It's not what she needed from me. She needed love. Support. Revenge just destroys, love is what builds. I want to love you and build a life with you. Forever."

"So do I." She threw herself into his arms, wrapped her own around his neck and kissed him. "So do I."

Emerson Maxfield knew without a shadow of a doubt, as her strong, handsome husband held her in his arms, that she was never going to be bored with her life again.

Because she knew now that it wasn't a party, a launch, a successful campaign that was going to bring happiness or decide who she was.

No, that came from inside of her.

And it was enough.

Who she was loved Holden McCall. And whatever came their way, it didn't scare her. Because they would face it together.

She remembered that feeling she'd had, adrift, like she had nowhere to go, like her whole life had been untethered.

But she had found who she was, she had found her heart, in him.

And she knew that she would never have to question where she belonged again. Because it was wherever he was.

Forever.

* * * * *

Read more from New York Times
*bestselling author Maisey Yates
and Harlequin Desire!*

Take Me, Cowboy
Seduce Me, Cowboy
Claim Me, Cowboy
Want Me, Cowboy
Need Me, Cowboy

#2701 DUTY OR DESIRE
The Westmoreland Legacy • by Brenda Jackson

Becoming guardian of his young niece is tough for Westmoreland neighbor Pete Higgins. But Myra Hollister, the irresistible new nanny with a dangerous past, pushes him to the brink. Will desire for the nanny distract him from duty to his niece?

#2702 TEMPTING THE TEXAN
Texas Cattleman's Club: Inheritance • by Maureen Child

When a family tragedy calls rancher Kellan Blackwood home to Royal, Texas, he's reunited with the woman he left behind, Irina Romanov. Can the secrets that drove them apart in the first place bring them back together?

#2703 THE RIVAL
Dynasties: Mesa Falls • by Joanne Rock

Media mogul Devon Salazar is suspicious of the seductive new tour guide at Mesa Falls Ranch. Sure enough, Regina Flores wants to take him down after his father destroyed her family. But attraction to her target might take her down first...

#2704 RED CARPET REDEMPTION
The Stewart Heirs • by Yahrah St. John

Dane Stewart is a Hollywood heartthrob with a devilish reputation. When a sperm bank mishap reveals he has a secret child with the beautiful but guarded Iris Turner, their intense chemistry surprises them both. Can this made-for-the-movies romance last?

#2705 ONE NIGHT TO RISK IT ALL
One Night • by Katherine Garbera

After a night of passion, Inigo Velasquez learns that socialite Marielle Bisset is the woman who ruined his sister's marriage. A staged seduction to avenge his sister might quell his moral outrage... But will it quench his desire for Marielle?

#2706 TWIN SCANDALS
The Pearl House • by Fiona Brand

Seeking payback against the man who dumped her, Sophie Messena switches places with her twin on a business trip with billionaire Ben Sabin. When they are stranded by a storm, their attraction surges. But will past scandals threaten their chance at a future?

SPECIAL EXCERPT FROM

New York Times *bestselling author Brenda Jackson welcomes you to Catalina Cove, where even the biggest heartbreaks can be healed...*

Read on for a sneak peek at
Finding Home Again...

A flash of pink moving around in his house made Kaegan frown when he recalled just who'd worn that particular color tonight. He glanced back at Sasha. "Tell Farley that I hope he starts feeling better. Good night." Without waiting for Sasha's response, he quickly walked off, heading inside his home.

He heard a noise coming from the kitchen. Moving quickly, he walked in to find Bryce Witherspoon on a ladder putting something in one of the cabinets. Anger, to a degree he hadn't felt in a long time, consumed him. Standing there in his kitchen on that ladder was the one and only woman he'd ever loved. The one woman he would risk his life for, and he recalled doing so once. She was the only woman who'd had his heart from the time they were in grade school. The only one he'd ever wanted to marry, have his babies. The only one who...

He realized he'd been standing there recalling things he preferred not remembering. What he should be remembering was that she was the woman who'd broken his heart. "What the hell are you doing in here, Bryce?"

His loud, booming voice startled her. She jerked around, lost her balance and came tumbling off the ladder. He rushed over and caught her in his arms before she could hit the floor. His chest tightened and his nerves, and a few other parts of his anatomy, kicked in the moment his hands and arms touched the body he used to know as well as his own. A body he'd introduced to passion. A body he'd—

"Put me down, Kaegan Chambray!"

He started to drop her, just for the hell of it. She was such a damn ingrate. "Next time I'll just let you fall on your ass," he snapped, placing her on her feet and trying not to notice how beautiful she was. Her eyes were a cross of hazel and moss green, and were adorned by long eyelashes. She had high cheekbones and shoulder-length curly brown hair. Her skin was a gorgeous honey brown and her lips, although at the moment curved in a frown, had always been one of her most noticeable traits.

PHBJEXP1119

"Let go of my hand, Kaegan!"

Her sharp tone made him realize he'd been standing there staring at her. He fought to regain his senses. "What are you doing, going through my cabinets?"

She rounded on him, tossing all that beautiful hair out of her face. "I was on that ladder putting your spices back in the cabinets."

He crossed his arms over his chest. "Why?"

"Because I was helping you tidy up after the party by putting things away."

She had to be kidding. "I don't need your help."

"Fine! I'll leave, then. You can take Vashti home."

Take Vashti home? What the hell was she talking about? He was about to ask when Vashti burst into the kitchen. "What in the world is going on? I heard the two of you yelling and screaming all the way in the bathroom."

Kaegan turned to Vashti. "What is she talking about, me taking you home? Where's Sawyer?"

"He got a call and had to leave. I asked Bryce to drop me off at home. I also asked her to assist me in helping you straighten up before we left."

"I don't need help."

Bryce rounded on him. "Why don't you tell her what you told me? Namely, that you don't need *my* help."

He had no problem doing that. Glancing back at Vashti, he said. "I don't need Bryce's help. Nor do I want it."

Bryce looked at Vashti. "I'm leaving. You either come with me now or he can take you home."

Vashti looked from one to the other and then threw up her hands in frustration. "I'm leaving with you, Bryce. I'll be out to the car in a minute."

When Bryce walked out of the kitchen, Kaegan turned to Vashti. "You had no right asking her to stay here after the party to do anything, Vashti. I don't want her here. The only reason I even invited her is because of you."

Kaegan had seen fire in Vashti's eyes before, but it had never been directed at him. Now it was. She crossed the room and he had a mind to take a step back, but he didn't. "I'm sick and tired of you acting like an ass where Bryce is concerned, Kaegan. When will you wake up and realize what you accused her of all those years ago is not true?"

He glared at her. "Oh? Is that what she told you? News flash—you weren't there, Vashti, and I know what I saw."

"Do you?"

"Yes. So, you can believe the lie she's telling you all you want, but I know what I saw that night."

Vashti drew in a deep breath. "Do you? Or do you only know what you think you saw?"

Then without saying anything else, she turned and walked out of the kitchen.

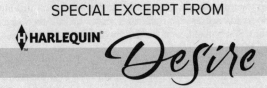
"That's it, Peterson Higgins, no more. You've had three servings already," Myra said, laughing, as she guarded the pan of peach cobbler on the counter.

He stood in front of her, grinning from ear to ear. "You should not have baked it so well. It was delicious."

"Thanks, but flattery won't get you any more peach cobbler tonight. You've had your limit."

He crossed his arms over his chest. "I could have you arrested, you know."

Crossing her arms over her own chest, she tilted her chin and couldn't stop grinning. "On what charge?"

The charge that immediately came to Pete's mind was that she was so darn beautiful. Irresistible. But he figured that was something he could not say.

She snapped her fingers in front of his face to reclaim his attention. "If you have to think that hard about a charge, then that means there isn't one."

"Oh, you'll be surprised what all I can do, Myra."

She tilted her head to the side as if to look at him better. "Do tell, Pete."

Her words—those three little words—made a full-blown attack on his senses. He drew in a shaky breath, then touched her chin. She blinked, as if startled by his touch. "How about 'do show,' Myra?"

Pete watched the way the lump formed in her throat and detected her shift in breathing. He could even hear the pounding of her heart. Damn, she smelled good, and she looked good, too. Always did.

"I'm not sure what 'do show' means," she said in a voice that was as shaky as his had been.

He tilted her chin up to gaze into her eyes, as well as to study the shape of her exquisite lips. "Then let me demonstrate, Ms. Hollister," he said, lowering his mouth to hers.

The moment he swept his tongue inside her mouth and tasted her, he was a goner. It took every ounce of strength he had to keep the kiss gentle when he wanted to devour her mouth with a hunger he felt all the way in his bones. A part of him wanted to take the kiss deeper, but then another part wanted to savor her taste. Honestly, either worked for him as long as she felt the passion between them.

He had wanted her from the moment he'd set eyes on her, but he'd fought the desire. He could no longer do that. He was a man known to forego his own needs and desires, but tonight he couldn't.

Whispering close to her ear, he said, "Peach cobbler isn't the only thing I could become addicted to, Myra."

Will their first kiss distract him from his duty?

Find out in
Duty or Desire
by New York Times *bestselling author Brenda Jackson.*

Available December 2019 wherever
Harlequin® Desire books and ebooks are sold.

Harlequin.com

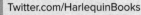

Love Harlequin romance?

DISCOVER.

Be the first to find out about promotions,
news and exclusive content!

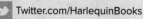
EXPLORE.

Sign up for the Harlequin e-newsletter and
download a free book from any series at
TryHarlequin.com.

CONNECT.

Join our Harlequin community to share
your thoughts and connect with other
romance readers!
Facebook.com/groups/HarlequinConnection

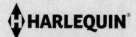

**ROMANCE WHEN
YOU NEED IT**

HSOCIAL2018